BIKER FUNERAL

The Father Barrett Files #1

JAMIE MASON

ROUGH
EDGES
PRESS

Biker Funeral
Paperback Edition
Copyright © 2022 Jamie Mason

Rough Edges Press
An Imprint of Wolfpack Publishing
5130 S. Fort Apache Rd. 215-380
Las Vegas, NV 89148

roughedgespress.com

Paperback ISBN 978-1-68549-142-0
eBook ISBN 978-1-68549-141-3
LCCN 2022942413

BIKER FUNERAL

"That which we call a reason for living can also be an excellent reason for dying."

– Albert Camus

Name That Tune

"SO HOW DID you end up here in Fulton, padre? You a kiddie-diddler or something?"

"No. I put a kiddie-diddler in the hospital."

Father Michael Barrett, SJ tossed off the rest of his beer and ordered another. He was enjoying a light buzz, his vision bleary and the bar room swimming gently in and out of focus. This was not a hard-core drunk like he habitually experienced alone with a box of wine at midnight, seeking the mouth of the black tunnel that made the world go away. But he decided it would do nicely for a Monday afternoon. His fifth beer came and he sipped.

"Put a kiddie-diddler in the hospital?" Gavin, Barrett's new best friend at the bar, seemed mildly surprised. "I thought priests took vows of non-violence."

"You betchya'. But I was a cop before I was a priest, so…"

Gavin narrowed his eyes, sipped his own drink and said nothing.

"I was never cut out for the whole parish scene,"

Barrett admitted. "Listening to people mumble and bitch during confession just wasn't my thing. But the Archbishop got wind of my background and you betchya' he recommended me to the Holy See. Congregation for the Doctrine of the Faith. I became an investigator."

Gavin considered this. "Interesting," he said quietly. "Go on."

The song on the canned music switched. Rolling piano chords, then a plaintive voice singing about a small-town girl living in her lonely world. The couple at the nearby table were arguing. Barrett grunted and hoisted his brew.

"I know this song," he said.

"Me, too," admitted Gavin. "Madonna, isn't it?"

"That's a guy singing."

Gavin cocked his head and listened. "Hunh, you're right," he said finally. "So, this investigator's gig. For the —what was it? Congregation?"

"Of the Doctrine of the Faith. What we once called the Inquisition. We investigate matters of canon law. Any time there's an issue like profanation of the sacraments, spreading of incorrect doctrine or professional misconduct…"

"Like kiddie-diddling."

"…like kiddie-diddling, we get involved."

"You think I want to hear that shit? Huh?"

Barrett winced and glanced over. The would-be cowboy arguing with his date had swept off his Stetson and was brandishing it. His date, a young redhead in lipstick and leather sat, head bowed demurely. Barrett allowed his gaze to linger a moment or two before resuming his story.

"I got sent to Portugal to investigate this bishop." He

swirled the beer in his glass and studied shapes in the foam. "You know a lot of priests hate this whole pedophile thing and fight it any way they can. But sometimes you get a bishop protecting somebody... It happens. And sometimes the bishop can even be involved himself. And then there was this one guy..."

Barrett looked down to hide his grimace.

"This was in the Diocese of... Well, a rural diocese, let's say. These people *cleaved* to the church. It was all they had. And the bishop, well. I got to hand it to him. He'd brought in a stable of good-looking, enthusiastic young priests. He'd gotten a bunch of programs off the ground, increased church attendance, youth involvement, applications to ministry—the works. The guy was, like, *Superbishop*."

A magical moment of silence fell in which the canned music, the groan of the ice machine and the arguing couple all stopped at once. With a click, the sound track shifted to pounding guitars, harmonies and a promise to meet you all the way.

"Now *this* one I recognize." Gavin repositioned his beer bottle on its little cardboard coaster. "Same guys who sang the song about Africa."

"That's them. Toto." Barrett nodded, half-listening, still chewing over memories of Portugal. "Anyway. When the kids started killing themselves, something ungodly like fifteen suicides in ten weeks, well...At first, the authorities had no idea what was going on. They were examining the phenomena across civil as opposed to ecumenical boundaries. But the church keeps an eye on that stuff, too. All the suicides were clustered within that one diocese."

The cowboy and his date were fighting again, their

voices rising. Barrett compensated by moving his stool closer to Gavin's.

"Turned out one of the kids had been molested by a priest so they sent me to investigate. I got the priest to confess. He rolled over on another priest who was doing the same thing. I checked and he *also* had a kid in his parish that'd offed himself. I forwarded my findings to the Curia. They interviewed the bishop and I started packing to go home. That's when the nun contacted me."

"See, one thing I never understood." Gavin scratched at the label on his bottle. "The Catholic Church never turns these people over to the police. They just—"

"Move them around. I know. *Believe* me, I know. It's—"

"I TOLD you I don't wanna HEAR that stuff!"

The cowboy was up on his feet now, the redhead rising to meet him. She reached out and touched his arm, but he shook it off. She tried again. This time he let her touch linger and seemed to calm down. He sighed and sat. The girl sat, too. They continued talking.

"It's a control thing." Barrett shot a sideways frown at the couple and then gestured for another beer. "The church is a law unto itself. Schools and educational institutions are more or less the same. They have these meta-judicial processes designed to impose what they call 'institutional justice.' As if *justice* is something that varies from institution to institution instead of being rooted in universal values like—"

"The Law."

Barrett could hear the capitalization and wondered if perhaps his new pal might be a retired lawyer or something. But that question, like a lot of other considerations, melted into the comfy drunk he was building. So he brushed it aside and continued.

"The nun's name was Sister Beatriz. Mexican. She transferred into the diocese same time the new bishop did. What was *interesting*." Barrett smacked a fist into his open palm. "Was that she transferred from the same diocese as him. So, she had some history on his Grace. And she'd been keeping track. Told me the man was poison. Begged me to do something. I had some holiday time coming—"

"Dammit, Jackie! That's not—"

"Randy, please!"

Barrett clenched his jaw. The youngsters were starting to piss him off.

"So, I took a few weeks off and stayed right where I was. Put on civilian clothes and kept digging…"

"*Civilian*?" Gavin chuckled. "That how you priests refer to us?"

"Certainly. We are the Army of God, after all…"

"Point taken." Gavin gestured with his beer bottle at the cowboy. "How much you wanna bet he beats her up?"

"Probably. She should leave."

"They never do."

"They never do." Barrett examined the girl a moment longer before resuming his story. "Anyhow, I started digging. Talked to the parents of the kids who had committed suicide. Turns out every single one had developed a 'special relationship' with their 'new' parish priest, every one of whom had 'taken an interest.' The kids, who had been universally bright and popular, all turned secretive. Reclusive. Almost overnight."

"That's what happens when kids are sexually abused."

"That's right." Barrett was surprised. "Gavin, were you a lawyer?"

"A *lawyer?* Fuck no!"

"A social worker, then."

At this, Gavin doubled over laughing. The voices of the cowboy and his date quieted. The music flipped again.

"Wow, must be Eighties night." Gavin indicated at the speaker behind the bar. "I thought they just played this one. Roxanna? Meet you all the way?"

"No, this is the Police."

"Great group!" Gavin toasted the guitar arpeggios and metronome beat of the new tune. "So let me jump ahead here. You figured out that Bishop X and his band of merry pedos had been working their way through the young people of that diocese in Portugal. You knew you couldn't get any action by confronting the bishop directly, so you… What?"

"Went to the archbishop." Barrett remembered it all distinctly. "I was packing to leave when the phone rang. Sister Beatriz calling to say she'd suddenly been transferred to Paraguay. One of the bishop's pet priests had been chosen as a sacrificial lamb and placed on administrative leave. And I was ordered back to Rome. Gavin, I…"

He stopped and gripped the edge of the bar. Clenched his teeth. Fought to keep his voice level despite the storm rising inside him. Barrett knew this storm, had ridden its waves of rage before. Behind these waves came a wind. And behind the wind, a darkness. For now he resisted.

"I couldn't fucking do it. I couldn't go back. Couldn't leave things the way they were."

"So, what did you do?"

The priest was still while the singer promised his girl the she didn't need to put on the red light or wear that dress tonight.

"Bishop liked tennis." Barrett's voice was bleak, sepulchral. "Used to drive into a club in Lisbon twice a month. Very new place. Run, surprisingly enough, by a gay couple. They had an entrance right from the second floor of an indoor parking garage. Which was where he parked his Mercedes the first and third Friday of every month between 8:17 and 8:38 PM. I checked, you see. The next Friday was the third Friday so I drove out and bought myself a ticket at 7:46 PM. Waited. And sure enough, he appeared. Stepped out of his jet-black Merc in his immaculate white tennies, shorts and polo shirt, like he always did."

Gavin sat very still, head bowed, listening with the kind of attentiveness Barrett associated with wolves, cougars, large, intelligent animals on the hunt. That's when he decided Gavin must be a hunter. That explained his stillness, his patient reticence.

"I wore a balaclava and orange mechanic's jumpsuit and brought along an old wooden Louisville Slugger. Little league edition. I didn't hesitate. Not even for a moment. Because by then I had the sworn depositions of three kids whom his Grace had personally *diddled.* My first swing was hard, aiming for the base of the skull. Wanted to disable or kill him. He happened to shrug and turn at that moment so the bat just shattered his shoulder blade. But next, I aimed for the face. See, by then he was down on one knee with his head exposed so I couldn't miss. No way. So I wound up and swung. Home run, you betchya'. Sub orbital eye socket and cheek bone shattered. *Pow!* Just shards and dust when I was done with the son-of-a-bitch."

Barrett's jaw clenched.

"You see...He *had* to be punished. God's punishment wasn't enough. He had to be punished by men. By his own. And what was more we had to be seen doing it. In the eyes of God and Law. He had to *answer.*"

"You didn't do any jail time?"

"Church fixed it. Same way they fix it for the pedos. I would be demoted. Re-assigned to parish duties. Moved. To here." Barrett toasted the municipality. "I was spared incarceration by the same institutional 'justice' that shielded that rotten. *Bastard.* Predatory. Son-of-a-bitch."

"Now, now." Gavin sipped his drink. "Let me buy you another. Oh, barkeep?"

"Oh, hey Gavin." The young, blond bearded man stepped up with a smile.

"Get my buddy the depressed priest another beer and a shot of Bushmill's. And you see that couple over there?"

"Randy and Jackie? Yeah."

"You send them a nice bottle of wine. From me. Okay?" Gavin laid a hand on the barman's wrist and said quietly, "I'm frankly a little worried, son."

"Right." The barman frowned, nodded and wiped the bar with a rag. "Want me to make a call?"

"No." Gavin clapped Barrett's shoulder. "The father here will do fine for back up. Won't you, father?"

"Fucking A." Barrett hoisted his empty glass. To the barman, he said: "Now, hop to."

As the kid pulled another pint, Barrett closed his eyes and breathed. The alcohol was making his stomach lurch. Upon reflection, he couldn't remember the last time he'd eaten. If he didn't put something in his stomach soon, the Bushmill's would put him over the line into blackout territory and he couldn't let that happen. He had e-mails to answer and parish "duties" (such as they were) to discharge. So, he went through his routine—same one he used whenever he found himself getting spinny with drink or experiencing the shakes that came from lack of it or found himself remembering the past. Sight, sound, and smell. He could see: the grainy wood of the bar beneath his elbow. Hear: the twanging guitars of a CCR tune. Smell: the slight odor of bleach, as ever-present on any bar-room floor as CCR on the juke.

There. He was coming back to himself now…

Glass shattered. From the corner of his eye, Barrett caught a blur of movement as the barman jumped back, wine bottle slipping from his fist because Randy had chosen that moment to hit Jackie. The sound of his hand smacking her face was a song Barrett knew better than any of the crap they'd been playing all afternoon. But by then he was on his feet and walking forward into that black tunnel—not the one that took the world away. The other one that took him into people's lives and changed them forever.

Games Without Frontiers

"HEY."

Randy looked up. He didn't see much. Just some asshole priest. Middle-aged, grey hair, kindly smile. Standing there like he was greeting parishioners at church on Sunday morning.

"Mind your own business," Randy spat.

Barrett smiled. "Now, is that any way to talk to someone who's just trying to help?"

"Fuck off, we don't need your help."

"Oh, but you do." Barrett's eyelids drooped to half-mast. "You do, my son."

"I'm not your son."

"You have fallen into error. Sin is upon you. Repent. Make your confession. Atone for your sins. I can help you. I'm a priest."

"You mean that's not a Halloween costume?" Randy —sallow-faced, blonde and grey-eyed—clenched a fist glimmering with swap-meet silver and turquoise rings. "I know you're the new priest, so I'mma be nice to you. Here in Fulton, we mind our own business."

"That so?"

"Especially between a man and his girl. This has nothing to do with you."

"Oh, I see. Well, thank you. Randy, is it? Thank you, Randy. I really appreciate your putting me in the picture about local customs. See, I've only been here a few weeks and don't know who's who or what's what yet, so it's right neighbourly of you. But if people mind their own business in Fulton, then how do they deal with riddles?"

"Huh?" Randy frowned.

"Yeah." Barrett rubbed his hands. "Riddles like: what do you call a jumped-up little cowboy cocksucker who gets off on smacking around little girls? Care to guess?"

Gavin got up from his bar-stool quietly and stood watching.

"Randy!" Barrett was beaming. "That's what you call someone like that. Now isn't that funny?"

Randy shook his head slowly back and forth, doubtless imitating some angry steer he'd seen in a cowboy movie. He took off his hat and set it on the table. Then he rose, all six feet ugly of him, spread his legs and raised his fists.

"I hate to do this to a priest," he admitted. "But you—"

Barrett kicked him savagely in the nuts—a textbook karate front-kick, delivered full-force. Randy doubled over with a yelp and Barrett kneed him in the face on the way down. Randy hit the floor, one hand holding his shattered nose, the other cupping his shrieking testicles.

"You're right, Randy." Barrett put his hands on his hips and looked down on the man. "You're *not* my son. My son would have some class, you betchya'. My son would be Catholic and wouldn't dare raise his hand to a man of the cloth, by God. You are some piece of work, I must say."

Barrett glanced over at Jackie, the little red-head, sitting there open-mouthed. "Excuse me, honey," he said, leaning over and lifting Randy's beer. He took a sip. "Ah, pale ale. I appreciate your taste, Randy. You at least have that going for you. But your anger issues are going to get you into serious trouble someday."

Barrett leaned against the table.

"You know what anger is, Randy? It's a sin. A grave one. Because anger is what happens when we put ourselves at the center of the world. And pretty soon we start seeing the world and all the people in it as ours, to do with as we please." Barrett took a deep swallow of pale ale and closed his eyes. The black tunnel was all around him now—that weird space from which he somehow talked from outside himself. He was never sure where the words came from. He just knew he was on a mission.

Gavin moved a step closer, dropped a hand into the pocket of his windbreaker and cocked his head.

Barrett opened his eyes. "See, Randy. We got one shot at this life. One chance to put ourselves right with God before He decides what to do with us. I am in serious dudgeon about the state of your soul, young man."

Randy, by this point slightly recovered, had moved to a sitting position, both hands on his nose, his butt against a chair leg. He was sitting forward, head between his raised knees and panting softly like a dog on a hot day.

"First thing." Barrett put down the beer with a *click* and began counting off on his fingers. "Get right with Man. How can you be right with God if you're not right with your fellow Man? Then? Make your contrition. Start with her. Is there anything you want to say to Jackie?"

Randy raised his eyes, blood-smeared fingers lingering around his lips. "Yeah," he mumbled.

"Well, good for you, bucko! Good for you." Barrett rubbed his hands. "What sweet, loving words of kindness and contrition do you have for this...*charming* young biker-lady?" He turned to the girl. "You *are* a biker-lady, aren't you? I would not dare presume your occupation or tribal affiliation, however your unique wardrobe would suggest you're not unfamiliar with the back seat of a Harley. Although not with Randy, here. Hey? He's more of a pick-up truck guy. So, pick-up truck guy. Speak! Tell Jackie what you have to say!"

Randy snuffled around blood and broken cartilage, wiped his face again and said to Jackie: "Fuck you, you two-timing fucking whore."

Gavin closed his eyes, lowered his face into his hand and shook his head slowly. Jackie, eyes on the table and head bowed, did not move while Barrett, meanwhile, had pushed out his lower lip and was nodding to himself.

"Of course. No other possible conclusion. You are in open rebellion against God, m'boy. Yea, verily. Thy soul is in mortal peril. I have no choice but to administer the sacraments."

He stepped forward.

"You—"

Randy lashed out with a furious kick at Barrett's knee that the priest managed to dodge. But the heel of Randy's boot (of course he wore boots!) grazed Barrett's shin. Then Randy was on his feet and grabbing a chair, swinging shoulder and hips, whipping the chair around in a blur. It scythed through the space Barrett had occupied just a moment earlier. When it finished its arc, Barrett rotated in, secured Randy's wrist and delivered a sharp elbow strike to the jaw, shattering it, putting Randy down again for good.

"*Dominos vobiscum, Et cum spiritu tuo,* my son." Barrett yanked the chair from Randy's desperate grasp, threw it aside and advanced. "Your sins are recognized. And forgiven. *Ego te absolvo.* In the name of the *Father...*"

Barrett hauled back and kicked Randy in the stomach so hard the air exploded from the kid's lungs.

"The *Son...*"

Barrett stomped Randy's hand, the bones splintering with a crunch. Randy loosed a mangled howl through his shattered mouth that was loud enough to shake the vault of heaven.

"And the Holy—"

It was far as Barrett got before a vast burning sensation seared his lower back and spread, at first unbearably hot and then plunging in temperature to freeze every muscle in his body and scramble his brain. He crashed to the floor.

"You can go ahead and make that call," Gavin said to the barkeep. Barrett felt handcuffs pinch his wrists. "Paramedics. Have them take Randy here to the hospital. Then swing by the detachment. Tell them I have one in the cells who's been tasered and needs follow-up."

———

BARRETT SLOUCHED in the back seat of Gavin's white Crown Victoria, shaking his head. The black tunnel was gone, leaving behind only bleariness, the last faint traces of drunkenness and a splitting headache.

"Amazing thing, isn't it?" Gavin, grinning at Barrett in the rear-view mirror, held up a little blue rectangle about the size of a TV remote. "Not exactly standard issue, but you can get them by mail-order from the States. Personal taser. I carry mine whenever I'm off duty."

"So you're a cop." Barrett's voice sounded low and dull, even to himself.

"Thirty years. Sergeant Gavin Lewis, RCMP at your service, padre. Must say. That was some performance you put on back there. Where'd you learn to fight like that?"

"Toronto." Barrett kicked himself for not pegging Lewis as a cop sooner. "Did six years as a general duty patrolman in the inner city."

"Yeah, I figured musta' been something like that. The way you laid the boots to that kid? Jesus." Lewis turned, his expression sympathetic. "Now don't get me wrong. I can't say he didn't have it coming. Randy is a raging shit-clown who's been terrorizing Fulton since he was a kid. Grew up to be a fine, upstanding citizen, as you can tell."

Barrett examined the rubber floor matting and said nothing.

"But you went too *far,* padre. See, I would have been content to let you knock him down a second time. But once it looked like you were going to end him, well…" Lewis twiddled his taser. "I had to step in in the interest of public safety, you understand."

Barrett clenched his teeth against the Taser hangover.

Lewis grinned. "I'm guessing that was your first ride on the taze."

"We didn't have them when I was on the force."

"They made us ride it when they introduced them

into our toolkit. It's a bitch." Lewis started the squad car. "We won't press charges, padre, and I won't forward any Randy brings. He's spending the night in the hospital. And you'll be spending the night in the cells. You're drunk and need to sober up anyway."

"You're drunk, too."

"Yeah but driving drunk is a perk of this job." Lewis pulled onto the street, narrowly missing a cyclist. He steered for the detachment.

You Owe Me One

BARRETT SHIVERED awake from the nightmare with a gasp. His dry sinuses, swollen feet and achy joints told him without even opening his eyes exactly where he was. *How…?* He scoured his memory until it came back: the bar, Lewis, the fight. The taser (he stiffened at the memory). He blinked. Abruptly sat upright, swinging his legs over the side of the hard bench where he'd slept and putting his feet to the concrete floor, remaining perpendicular with hands on either side to steady himself on the bench while his brain reeled.

"Well! There's Sleeping Beauty." Lewis appeared outside the bars with a tin cup of coffee. "Wasn't sure when you'd be waking up."

Barrett accepted the coffee through the meal slot, sipped and studied the antiquated squad-room of Lewis' tiny rural detachment. One- and two-man posts were almost entirely a thing of the past, but Barrett could tell by the Government of Canada® signage that the federal bean-counters had pinched pennies by crowding the

RCMP and Conservation Service together in the same headquarters. Lewis noticed him noticing.

"Yeah. Me and Walton, the CO, back each other up, share expenses, office space. Plenty of poachers wind up in there." Lewis reached into a pocket, produced a flask and held it up. "You care for some cream in your coffee, sir?"

"God, yes." Barrett thrust the cup out and sighed as Lewis poured a healthy tot of whiskey into his brew. He sipped and felt the shakes still within him.

"You owe me one, padre." Lewis produced keys and unlocked the cell. Barrett followed him to the desk and dropped into one of the guest chairs. Lewis took a seat behind the workspace piled high with memo envelopes, evidence bags and stacks of newsprint. "You're free and clear. No charges pressed, no entry into the national criminal database. You're golden. But." The Mountie dragged his own mug over, seasoned it from the flask and toasted Barrett. "You owe me."

"Sure…" Barrett, feeling agreeable, shrugged in a friendly way. "I mean, I'm not sure what—"

"You're an ex-cop who can handle himself in a fight. Around here, that's useful. You've also got some investigative background. Never know when that might come in handy. I may tap you to help us out on the odd job or two. This in return for what I did for you this morning."

Barrett waited.

"Your…*boss* called."

Oh, Christ, no. Not Archbishop Crowe…

"Archbishop Crowe from the Grand Diocese of Vancouver. Called the detachment out of concern when you failed to dial in to a phone conference yesterday. Unfortunately, Walton was on duty. He explained that you were in the cells. He went thin on details so when I called back, I was able to put things in the best possible light. I explained that you had assaulted a man who was attacking a woman. Told him you were being held as a matter of routine procedure. Didn't mention public drunkenness, assault or excessive cruelty. Spun it as best I could. You owe me."

Barrett had to agree: he *did* owe Lewis.

"Despite that," Lewis continued, "he has instructed you to present yourself at the Campbell River airport this afternoon at five. He's taking a charter flight in from Vancouver. Sorry, hoss. Did my best for you, but he's mucho pissed."

To Barrett's surprise, Lewis reached back behind a coat stand and drew out a battered nylon string guitar. He laid it over his knee and fiddled with the tuning pegs briefly. Then he played the opening arpeggios of *If You Could Read My Mind* by Gordon Lightfoot.

"I hate that song," muttered Barrett and sipped, recalling his nightmare about pianos.

———

BARRETT STEPPED out of the detachment, grappled a pair of Ray-Bans from his coat pocket and pushed them into place against the ungodly glare of the noontime sun. With a groan, he bent his steps toward the parish house and began walking.

Fulton, he reflected, stepping off a curb by the convenience store, was urban blight in the middle of more or less pristine wilderness. The town sat on the shores of Upper Campbell Lake near Strathcona Park Lodge, halfway between Campbell River and Gold River. Once upon a time, it had been a pretty tourist destination, a favored weekend getaway spot. But time and a hollowed-out economy—to say nothing of an opioid crisis—had transformed the jolly ice-cream dishing, souvenir-hawking, tourist-catering town into a concrete hole, a slum of inhabited ruins surrounded by First Nations communities that were just government-issue houses draped with an aura of despair. The government was the main employer for non-Indians and small businesses fluctuated in and out of existence like photographic images in developing solution.

This is dead land, Barrett reflected as a herd of Native youth on bikes appeared on the sidewalk ahead. *This is cactus land.* 'The Hollow Men' by T.S. Eliot was weirdly fitting for this town barely clinging to life on the edge of the first quarter of the twenty-first century.

The swarm of Native kids hurtled toward him. Barrett recognized a few. They were a mix of fourteen to sixteen-year old boys and girls, alike in their black hoodies and glares of flat resentment. One spat on the pavement close by his shoe as they blew past. Another said something indistinct and the group erupted into jeering hoots as it coasted away. Barrett stopped where he was on the sidewalk and watched them go.

Kids like that were exactly the type taken advantage of by those priests he had spent nine years chasing for the Curia. Each case always followed the same pattern: vulnerable, trusting youth being enfolded by an all-embracing church and then being taken advantage of by priests who were outwardly pious but inwardly perverse, and equipped with a lust that would make an ancient Roman blush. In *The Duino Elegies,* Rilke had spoken of blades secreted within the wings of angels. A sympathetic critic might conflate those wings with the Church and the blades with the poisoned priests who molested children. But Barrett wondered what *kind* of Church would allow blades to remain within its wings in the first place. The failure to find an answer, and the revulsion he felt at the answers he *did* find had piled up within him until he could stand it no longer.

His was not to reason why. But it had grown impossible for him to do or die. Not anymore.

The spire of St. Michael's and St. Joan's Catholic Church appeared ahead. Once upon a time, the Church had done a bustling ministry with the local Natives. Nowadays the congregation numbered perhaps thirty, all white, all poor, all due to die sometime in the next decade. Barrett's appointment here included the tacit understanding that it might become his responsibility to shut down the parish for good someday soon.

He approached the sagging A-frame of the church. Its outer glass wall was smudged and stained, its roof tiles mis-matched and missing in patches, its landscaping overgrown despite the cold November air. He took the narrow flagstone path that wound around the building to the narrow stairwell cut into the walkway. He descended the steps to his office door. Letting himself in, he flicked on the light, dropped into his chair and warmed up the computer while sorting through mail. Bills, bills, bills…

Tossing the envelopes aside, he dialled voicemail on the parish handset and listened to messages as his tired PC's screen glowed to life.

"Father Barrett, this is Brother Steven, the Archbishop's personal assistant. Wondering why you're not on the weekly counselling call…"

Barrett deleted that message.

"Father Barrett, Brother Steven again. You—"

Delete.

"Father Barrett, Brother Ste—"

Delete. A hang up call. Then…

"Father Barrett, this is Archbishop Crowe. You will report to me immediately upon your release from custody by the RCMP. I will be at the Campbell River airport this evening at five o'clock. You're to present yourself to me punctually in the executive lounge for a professional reassessment and examen. You will refrain from exercising any of your duties as parish priest of St. Michael's and St. Joan's until that time. Dominus vobiscum."

Barrett raised his eyebrows. *Alrighty, then.* With that, he deleted the last voicemail, switched off his computer and left the office, mounting the steps to the flagstone path and following it around to the rear parking lot. At the opposite end of the vast, empty lot, a fifth wheel, sides weathered and wheels sagging, mouldered in the shade of an overhanging oak. It seemed as much a part of the landscape as the roots and soils themselves. The door above the air-stairs opened and a thin-faced man wearing a ball-cap poked his head out.

"Hello, father! Was just going to open a beer. Care for one?"

"You betchya', Scooter." Barrett tugged off his tweed jacket and slung it over a shoulder. Scooter disappeared briefly before returning clutching two cold, sweating cans of Lucky Lager. He descended to join Barrett at the umbrella table with the scuffed laminate surface.

"Here you be, father."

"Thanks." Barrett cracked the tab. "Wish me luck. I've been called up on the carpet."

"By your superiors? Yeah, well. Fuck 'em." Scooter took a seat in the other lawn chair and took a deep swallow of beer. "Used to be real impressed with bishops and monsignors and suchlike. Now after eight years parked back here taking care of St Mike's & Jo's, I know that all bosses are assholes to one extent or another."

"What about Crowe?"

"Archbishop Crowe of Vancouver?" Scooter chuckled. "He's been in the chair for five years, now. You, by comparison, have been here about as many *weeks*. Crowe is a dictator of the old school."

"Like Idi Amin?"

"More like Josef Stalin. I swear, if that asshole had a guillotine he'd use it." Scooter checked his watch. "The last guy we had here only lasted a year. Spent the last three months of it on convalescent leave. Job-related stress. They brought in Father Dolan to pinch hit. He was lined up to take over until you showed up. He none too pleased upon learning of your arrival."

"Father Dolan?"

"He's been second string at the cathedral in Victoria forever. Guy gets routinely passed over for parish assignments for some reason. Has his heart set on our little church here in Fulton."

"So he's frustrated."

"Psychotically so. Well, fuck him. I don't like him much. He's a climber. Can't stand those try-hards. He's a grade-A snitch and a kiss-ass, too. Kind of a weirdo."

Barrett filed away the information. Accepted a second beer when Scooter ducked inside and returned with two more.

"I spent the night in lock-up," Barrett admitted. "Drunkenness. And an assault. Kid named Randy. He was beating up his girl, a young woman named Jackie. I stepped in. Laid the boots to Randy."

"Oh, Jackie!" Scooter rapped the table emphatically. "You stepped in to save Jackie? You know she's *Mick's* daughter?"

"Mick?"

"Sure! Big Mick Hudson! Ho ho, padre." Scooter tilted his beer can and drank. "You've got yourself hooked up with the cream of the Fulton underworld! Big Mick is the president of the Paladins."

"The motorcycle gang?" Barrett's temples were throbbing again.

"One and the same." Scooter shook his head. "Man. You *saved* the daughter of the Paladins' president? Big Mick owes you now. He's gonna be generous!"

"Well, I'm not really inclined to accept any sort of—"

"Bullshit. Accept it. Or he'll break your fucking legs."

"Oh." Barrett frowned. "Scooter, what time is it?"

"About one."

Barrett downed the second beer but gestured for Scooter to sit.

"I got time to grab a shower before the drive to Campbell River. Watch out for the place while I'm gone?"

"Always do."

"Thanks."

Scooter watched Barrett cross the lot and disappear down the narrow flagstone path. Barrett was the fifth pastor he had served in his eight years here and Scooter liked him better than most. Barrett seemed authentic. And more than a little tortured.

———

BARRETT PAUSED AMONG THE TREES, momentarily overcome by stress, the headache, the light-headedness of drink on an empty stomach and memories of his nightmare.

The piano…

It had haunted him since his earliest days. The merest shadow of one caused the horrifying images from his nightmares to loom large in his waking mind. He'd grown up beneath the vast shadow of a grand piano that had dominated their front room, a room also filled with the shadows of men, a whispered conspiracy of dark trench-coats that came and went, men smoking and muttering and carrying guns. That forest of legs and shoes, the shadow and refuge of the nightmarish piano caused him to turn out a certain way, along a rebellious path that required an iron spine.

He'd joined the police.

Then the Jesuits.

He'd chosen his side.

Excellency

BARRETT STEERED the parish Hyundai along Gold River Highway, winding between tiered rock and ranks of solemn firs guarding the road to Campbell River. This section of Vancouver Island was still heavily forested, with no sign of the stunted mange left by constant clear-cutting and reforestation. Barrett wondered how long this paradise would last. *Sooner or later,* he thought, *everything winds up on the auction block.* Even priests.

His life as an investigator for the Holy See had meant living mostly out of a suitcase. Barrett had lost count of the number of times he'd pulled into some airport or train station, found lodgings and dropped anchor for a period of time. Inevitably he dealt with the Four Horsemen of small communities: suspicion, hostility, ignorance, indifference. He was accustomed to floating through groups, interacting with them in the most superficial ways and departing with relief. Because six years as a cop had taught Barrett to distrust people. Now, with this assignment in Fulton, he was expected to...

To *what?* Integrate? Barrett jammed a cigarette in his mouth and lit up. Making him a parish priest, forcing him to actually *minister* to people with whom he had absolutely nothing in common was possibly the worst imaginable misuse of his talents. Of course, he was expected to immediately acquiesce, to simply accept the decisions of his superiors as more or less indistinguishable from the will of God. This was, for Barrett, the most annoying aspect of Roman Catholic professional culture. But he had to admit, a stroke of genius where labor relations were concerned.

Archbishop Crowe had taken an instant dislike to Barrett. Most people did. Barrett had read an article about how people who are self-sufficient (or who seem to be) elicit the dislike of others. He had seen it in the small communities through which he passed. It was the same where bosses and bureaucrats were concerned—bosses and bureaucrats all inhabiting, in his experience, the world's smallest town with the narrowest possible horizon of achievement…

Empire building.

Barrett's sigh welled up in a fog of disgust and cigarette smoke, clouding the windshield as he turned into the Campbell River airport parking lot. To his annoyance, the brightly-colored lot sign advised him that the least amount of time for which he could purchase a feasible parking ticket was three (3) hours and cost forty (40) dollars. Barrett gritted his teeth, fed his credit card into the slot and grumbled when the robot attendant stuck out its paper tongue at him. Forty bucks down the drain. And because Crowe refused his reimbursements as a matter of course, Barrett knew it was money he could kiss goodbye.

A security guard accosted him as he entered the small

terminal building. "Father Barrett?" The guard smiled. "There's no smoking in the terminal, sir…"

"Oh. Sorry." Barrett stepped back outside and ground his cigarette underfoot. "My last airport meeting was in Calcutta…"

"No problem, sir. Archbishop Crowe is waiting for you in the executive lounge."

"I was afraid you were going to say that."

"This way, sir."

Barrett followed the guard across the industrial granite flooring to a narrow set of four carpeted steps that ended at a velvet rope attended by a Commission-aire. The attendant unclipped the rope and admitted Barrett to the seating area of a lounge unoccupied by any save a single customer.

Archbishop Andrew Crowe of the Archdiocese of Vancouver was an organization man to his bones. Thin-faced, sere, balding and bespectacled, he seemed to exist in a permanent cloud of administrative processes and paperwork. It occurred to Barrett that he had never seen Crowe *not* surrounded by piles of file folders, or without his ever-present red felt-tip pen.

"Father Barrett." Archbishop Crowe looked up, red felt-tip hovering over a document. "How are you?"

It was Crowe's favorite opening move: a polite pleas-antry, just the right words but uttered in a tone of abso-lute, soul-deadening indifference. Barrett smiled patiently, reminded himself of the Four Horsemen and responded: "I am well, Archbishop, thank you for asking."

"Thanks be to *God,*" Crowe corrected him, capping his pen and moving his papers to one side. He gestured for Barrett to take a seat across the table from him. A waiter coasted up. Crowe said: "I will have a glass of orange juice, please. And nothing for my friend."

Prick. Barrett considered lighting a cigarette but decided against it. The waiter nodded and coasted away.

"So. How are you?" Again, the flat, soulless tone.

"I am well, Archbishop. Thanks be to *God.*"

"*Good.* Good." Crowe held Barrett's gaze blankly for a few seconds before turning to the lounge window. "But of course everything *isn't* well or I wouldn't be here. I have only ever been told that a priest of mine was in jail once before, and that was due to a protest over oil pipelines. Perfectly acceptable, of course. There has always been a streak of fashionable resistance running through the more liberal quarters of our church. That sort of thing is understandable. Laudable, even. However."

Archbishop Crowe paused while his orange juice was delivered. The waiter glanced at Barrett, noted Crowe's frown of displeasure and retreated.

"You will be pleased to know," Crowe continued, sipping, "that Bishop Olmos is expected to make a complete recovery. Or, near complete. Facial reconstruction surgery, I am told, can be quite involved. Apparently, there will be a period of therapy and convalescence."

"I'm very pleased to hear that, Archbishop."

Crowe hesitated, considering whether or not to address Barrett's flippant pleasantry and its timing within the flow of his remarks. Barrett noted these deliberations and suppressed a chuckle. At length, Crowe elected to plunge ahead.

"When I received the telephone call from the Curia indicating that you were joining the Archdiocese, I admit I had misgivings. But, of course, we are enjoined to practice forgiveness. I was counselled to see my role as offering you a 'second chance.' Which I have done."

"Thank you, your Excellency."

"Which the *Church* has done."

"Thanks be to God."

"In the name of whose authority I speak now."

"Yes, your Excellency."

Crowe sighed. "What happened?"

"Archbishop, a young woman in our community was being bullied and physically abused. I stepped in and –"

"And lost control?"

"Ah, not exactly…"

"Then what? Exactly."

"Well, my initial goal, your Excellency, was just to intervene and restrain. But the young man wouldn't respond to Christian redirection. He became violent."

"And you, rather than turn the other cheek and control yourself, responded in kind. I understand the man was sent to hospital."

"Apparently so, Archbishop."

"Apparently? You didn't attend?"

"No, I was indisposed."

"Indisposed?"

"Uh, in handcuffs."

Crowe breathed a long, sharp inhale. "You got violent with the police, as well?"

"Oh, no!" Barrett raised his hands. "No, your Excellency. I didn't get the chance. I mean…Well, you see. They tazed me."

"'Tazed'?"

"Deployed an energy weapon that shocks on contact and—"

"They tasered you. I see." Crowe narrowed his eyes. "Why would they have to do that, Father Barrett?"

"I honestly don't know, Archbishop."

"Could it be that you failed to *respond* to lawful redirection?"

"I never got the chance, your Excellency."

"I see." Crowe was obviously done. He broke visual contact with Barrett and flipped open a folder on the stack beside him. "Well, congratulations are in order. I've never seen a more meteoric rise or spectacular plunge in a priest's career. In the space of one year you've gone from doing investigations for the Holy See to actually *being* investigated by the police. You've certainly had a checkered past. You have a temper. You're demonstrably violent. It says here you were ordered to seek counselling for alcohol addiction by your superiors in the Curia."

"Yes, your Excellency."

"Did you?"

"Yes, your Excellency."

"Drinking under control?"

"Certainly, Archbishop." *I never spill a drop,* Barrett added mentally.

"Good." Crowe paged through the contents of the folder. "So. Received into the archdiocese…Initial evaluation…Professional counselling and discussion with Monsignor Wright…and then assignment to Fulton. Parish of St. Michael's and St. Joan's. How's church attendance?"

"Ah, poor. The Anglicans fare much better."

"No surprise there. They usually do in that part of the island. They've been pressuring me to close down the church in Fulton for a while."

Barrett said nothing.

Crowe was examining him now, eyes crawling over every inch of Barrett. If Barrett didn't know better, he would imagine some sort of sensual interest in him. But

Crowe, so far as he could tell, didn't share the priest-hood's predilection toward homosexuality. Since the Archbishop's sole area of erotic interest seemed to lie in the accrual of administrative power, his gaze was more like that of a butcher sizing up a side of beef on the chopping block.

"I'm going to relieve you of your parish duties, Father Barrett." Crowe's tone was soft. Not gentle, exactly, but tender. *Like a man anticipating and then relishing execution of a treasured duty*, Barrett thought. "You will be placed on administrative leave—with pay. I am also going to proscribe another consultation with Monsignor Wright for the purpose of professional re-evaluation. So long as you are with us, we want to find the optimal position in the Archdiocese to facilitate best use of your talents."

"Yes, your Excellency."

Crowe began packing up his papers. "You will be replaced by Father Dolan from Victoria. He knows the parish. Has covered for us there before. I'll telephone him this evening from Vancouver. He'll be along in a day or two. Until then, you're not to hold services, attend to parochial duties or administer the sacraments. Is that clear?"

"Very clear, Archbishop."

"Good. Keep your head down. Keep your nose clean. I'll be praying for you. That's all." Crowe buried his nose in a folder.

"Thank you, your Excellency."

Barrett rose and made for the door. He glanced back just once to see Crowe uncap his red felt-tip and resume work. Barrett experienced the same cold flush of rage he remembered feeling when called on the carpet by police administration—that filthy sense of being judged by those he privately considered lesser men. Precinct captains, commissioners, bishops and archbishops: they were all the same. Servants of a bureaucracy that served no purpose other than to perpetuate its own existence. Suppressing a tremor of rage, he stepped from the lounge, jamming a cigarette in his mouth. He had his lighter in hand, ready to go the moment he stepped from the terminal building.

———

HE FOUND a liquor store near the highway and bought himself a six-pack, a fresh deck of smokes and some chewing gum. Standing in line behind a young couple, he wondered how Randy was doing in the hospital and what Jackie would be up to these days. He wouldn't be surprised to hear she was probably visiting him, moved to pity by the beating Barrett had inflicted on him. He had seen it before: battered women who felt sorry for their batterers. Women, he reflected, were every bit as puzzling and opaque as church administrators. Barrett paid for his purchases and got behind the wheel of the Hyundai. Once outside of city limits, he cracked open the first can and sipped as he settled in for the long drive back to Fulton.

Sacrament

BARRETT WAS SIX. He was hiding under the piano. He could see the legs of adults…

BAM! BAM! BAM!

The men wore patent leather shoes and the women, stockings and high heels and everyone held a drink…

BAM! BAM! "HEY, FATHER! WAKE UP!"

…and he…

"YOU IN THERE?"

Barrett tilted upright in bed, eyes aching, head pulsing, his bladder full and his anger rising at whoever was pounding on the parish house door with what sounded like a sledgehammer at—

"FATHER!"

(he glanced at the clock)

BAM! BAM!

—three in the morning.

Having not reached REM sleep and still half-drunk, he lurched in bare feet to the chair over which he'd thrown his housecoat, untangled and threw it around his shoulders before stumbling to the entrance hall. Pausing to flick on the outside light, through the window Barrett could discern the shapes of two men on the parish house stoop. He unlocked and opened the door a crack.

"You Father Barrett?" The man spoke from behind a huge grey beard, his long grey hair held in place by a headband and he wore dark glasses although it was night. Barrett noted the leather vest, the jeans and black work boots. The speaker and his smaller, thinner companion looked like they had both stepped out of a Harley Davidson commercial.

"Yes, I'm Michael Barrett." He blinked. "What can I do for you?"

The bearded man grinned broadly and tugged off his sunglasses. "Well goddam, padre!" He stuck out a paw. "Let me be the first to shake your hand! Goddam. It's an honor to meet the man who put the little fucker who hit Jackie in hospital. Name's Pappy, Vice-President of the Paladin's Motorcycle Club and Jackie's uncle. Come on down to the clubhouse. Big Mick wants to speak to you."

"It's three in the morning."

"Perfect time! C'mon get your clothes on."

"Well, look, I can't."

"But you *have* to!" Rather than threatening, the man's expression was one of genuine surprise. "Big Mick says so."

"He does, huh?" Barrett sighed. If it was just this bearded yo-yo and his side-kick, he could have seen them off by himself. But he knew from experience that bikers were like hornets or nuns. If you got on the wrong side of one or more, the rest could swarm and make your life miserable.

"Okay. Give me a sec."

"That's the spirit!"

Twenty minutes later, arms wrapped around Pappy's waist, clutching the Harley's chassis for dear life between his knees, Barrett hurtled along Fulton's main drag. He wasn't sure what made him more uncomfortable, the prospect of imminent death as Pappy accelerated onto the highway or the feeling of clutching a hairy biker in his arms. As it stood, he just had to grit his teeth and bear it. Which he did for another twenty minutes as they slalomed down a few miles of the Trans-Canada before turning off onto a logging road. Pappy switched on the high-beams as they coasted along the dips and curves of a well-maintained trail through the woods until ending on a paved access road. Pappy swerved onto the blacktop and, five minutes later, they were slowing and turning into a compound.

Barrett alighted clumsily, then stretched and looked around. He spied a large metal Quonset hut structure and two houses, one of which looked abandoned, its front yard littered with vehicles in various stages of disassembly. There were lights and music coming from the open garage door of the second house. Pappy clapped Barrett's shoulder and led him toward the din.

"I know that song," Barrett said. "AC/DC isn't it?"

"Good old metal, you bet." Pappy ushered him across the threshold onto the concrete nap of the garage floor and across to the carpeting. "Hey, Mick! Look who's here!"

The three-car garage was carpeted in what Barrett recognized as a Persian-style area rug. Scattered across it, from doorway to the huge mechanic's work-bench in back, were scuffed sofas and coffee tables. Barrett also noted two beer kegs and the portable CD player from which the singer was screeching about riding the highway to hell. Barrett uneasily eyed the dozen or so bikers lounging around on the furniture like a pack of lazy but lethal hounds. At a gesture from one of them, Jackie detached herself from the wall and switched off the CD player.

"Well, there he is!"

A fatter, younger version of Pappy burst through a doorway in the rear hauling another keg. He positioned it by the end of the nearest couch, obliging a bald dude with face tattoos to move his legs, which he did with a muttered, "Sorry, Mick." Big Mick set the keg down with a crash, tapped it with a nozzle and sprayed foamy beer into a red plastic cup, which he thrust into Barrett's hands.

"Man, father! It's an honor. Truly. Jackie! Get the father a chair, will ya? Fuck, it's good to see you." Big Mick wrapped his arm around Barrett's shoulders and gave a squeeze that flattened Barrett's lungs and induced a dizzying vertigo. "You saved my little girl! You saved Jackie from another beating by that no-good Randy son-of-a-bitch. Sorry, Jack. No disrespect about your mother."

"None taken." A lanky man with long sideburns and grey eyes hoisted his cup. "My brother's a shit-bag. Got what he deserved."

Barrett sipped his beer. Nodded. And tried to smile like he was at ease (which he was not). Jackie appeared, bearing one of those improbably comfy fold-out chairs in a Canadian flag pattern. Barrett lowered himself cautiously, noting her red eyes and mascara-stained cheeks. She had recently unburdened herself of a good cry and looked poised to have another at any moment.

"How are you, Jackie?" he muttered. "Everything okay?"

"No." She spat the word sullenly, turned on her heel and stalked off.

Big Mick laughed. "My little girl! So *emotional*. We used to think maybe she could be an actress. Like, save up a bunch of money and send her to acting school. That's a real thing, right? Acting school?"

"Sure." Barrett gulped shitty beer that left a formaldehyde aftertaste. "You're talking a fine arts education."

"Exactly!" Big Mick beamed. "He's a smart guy, ain't he, fellas?"

"He's alright," allowed Jack.

"Sure he is," muttered the bald guy with the face tattoos. Pappy and his companion beamed.

"We owe you." Big Mick laid a hand on Barrett's shoulder, gazing into the priest's eyes meaningfully. "*I* owe you. And I'm never going to forget that."

"Well…" Barrett shifted uncomfortably and glanced at where Jackie sulked, head down, in a corner. "You don't really owe me any—"

"*BULLSHIT.* Pardon the language, padre, but you've done a solid for the Paladins. Whether or not you like it, by the Code, we're indebted to you. That's a serious thing to the brotherhood of the road, father."

"I…" He cleared his throat. "I imagine it would be, yes."

"So." Big Mick clapped the shoulder again, firmly this time, and drew Barrett toward a narrow door in the rear wall of the garage. "We're allies. And we're going to do you a solid, pops. Count on it. But first." He paused, chuckled and shook his head. "First, we're actually gonna *impose* and ask another favor of you. Isn't it funny how things are often like it, that way? Ya' know. People come into your life with generosity and you just can't help asking: can you do just one more thing for me?" He laughed and the half-dozen or so Paladins joined him.

"Well, sure. I guess." He ambled behind Big Mick toward the narrow doorway. "If it's in my power…"

The door opened onto a windowless concrete room. Mick switched on the lights. Empty steel shelving lined three walls. There was something under a sleeping bag on a table in the center of the room. Pappy stepped in behind Barrett and shut the door. Big Mick moved to the table and grasped the top edge of the sleeping bag. "So, ah. About Randy…" Big Mick pulled back the sleeping bag. And there was Randy. Pale. White. Not breathing. With a black hole in the center of his forehead.

———

BARRETT WASN'T sure how much time passed in a disoriented blur. As a clergyman, he was accustomed to dead bodies. He'd helped tend to several. But not the dead bodies of fit, healthy people with whom he had been speaking just the day before. Big Mick's voice coalesced out of the rush of blood in his ears, coming back in dribs and drabs, at first.

"…later…found out…hospital. And was released this evening." Big Mick paused. "He, ah, met with an accident on the way home. A *traffic* accident."

"I can see that," said Barrett, fixated on the bullet hole between Randy's eyebrows.

"Helluva tragedy," muttered Pappy.

"I'll say!" Big Mick shook his head. "Thing is—one of our guys did it."

"Oh?"

"Yeah. See, Randy was going through a cross-walk, and…"

"I get the picture."

"Thing is, we don't want our guy to lose points on his license because of the accident. You understand."

"Oh yes. I'd say it's pretty clear to me, Mick."

"Good." Mick wrapped his arm around Barrett's shoulders again and steered him toward the door. Pappy stepped past them and covered Randy's body with the sleeping bag again. Mick paused a few steps from the door and said to Barrett, "We need to give him a decent burial. Me? I just wanted to leave him for the buzzards but Jackie wouldn't allow it. She's a total mess over all this."

"Sure."

"It's the least I can do for her."

Before Barrett could open his mouth to say that he was no longer a practicing clergyman, that he was specifically prohibited from delivering any of the sacraments and couldn't help them, Big Mick pulled an envelope out of his pocket and pushed it into Barrett's hands. Barrett pulled open the flap and riffled a stack of hundred-dollar bills with his thumb.

"There's five grand in there," said Mick. "Think of it as a donation."

Barrett, realizing that his present status conferred upon him no immediate obligation to donate the money to the church, pocketed the envelope with a neutral expression.

———

BARRETT SAT beside Jackie in the cab of the pick-up truck. Pappy was at the wheel.

"Jackie," Pappy said, "you should have something to eat. You'll feel better."

"Jack just killed Randy and you thinking eating is gonna make me feel better?"

"Well it couldn't hurt, sweetheart."

"Jackie," Barrett said quietly. "There's no way to console you for the pain you're going through. Words are never good enough, and nothing anybody else feels or says can make a difference when you're lost. I get it. All we can do is be here for each other. And I'll be here for you. And your family. I'm awful sorry, honey."

In the dim dashboard light, Pappy smiled.

"Thank you," whispered Jackie.

The access road cut deep into the Agricultural Land Reserve. The forests of western Canada, sprawling and remote, closed around them like a shroud until the nearest light from any city was swallowed in a starry, infinite sky. The snarl of bikes filled the air behind them. Their tight little convoy was going out beyond range of the deepest RCMP and Conservation patrols—out into a no-man's-land of vast woods untrammeled, in some places, by human feet for decades.

They rode for an hour before pulling onto a logging road. Big Mick and the rest of his gang parked their bikes and heaved Randy, rolled in a carpet, out of the truck and set him on their shoulders.

I guess I'm up, Barrett thought. As was customary on clerical visits, he had left the house with his Bible and so had it with him now. He took up his place at the head of the procession.

"We're heading into the woods here, father," said Pappy somberly. "We'll shine a light up ahead."

Barrett nodded. They set off down the path into the dark forest, the sound of Jackie's sobs hovering in the night like owls. They walked, by Barrett's estimation, close to two miles into the woods, stumbling over gopher holes and the great, raised ribs of old growth tree-roots snarling the ground. Eventually, they came to a small clearing where Big Mick called a halt. Three of the bikers attacked the soft earth with shovels while Barrett and the others watched. Soon they had dug a hole three feet deep, wide and long enough to accommodate the corpse of a grown man. The pall bearers set the rolled carpet containing Randy down by the hole.

"Okay, padre," said Big Mick quietly. "You're on."

Barrett performed the sacrament. One of the bikers held a flashlight so he could read. John 11:25, the resurrection and the life and the story of Lazarus being raised from the dead. Jackie stood, supported between Pappy and Big Mick as Barrett spoke, stone-faced throughout. At one point, he paused.

"Does anyone have anything they want to say about the deceased?"

A lengthy silence passed. No one spoke.

Barrett considered the rolled carpet. *Poor bastard,* he thought. Was there anything more pathetic than a man dying and being buried in an unmarked grave, mourned by no one? If so, Barrett couldn't imagine it.

On impulse, he knelt, fished his St. Ignatius medal out from under his shirt and removed it, placing it in the pocket of Randy's shirt. Then he stood and gestured for the body to be lowered.

Number One

BLEARY FROM A LACK of sleep and the two beers he'd had with breakfast, Barrett halted his shopping cart by the dairy freezer and leaned on the handle, studying the dizzying array of eggs and cheeses on offer. Reminding himself he had an extra $5,000 to play with, he opted for the high-end, gourmet cheddar and dropped it into his cart before wheeling over to the deli section.

Fourteen-dollar bacon, he thought. He'd always wanted to try the fourteen-dollar bacon. Barrett reached out and grasped a package. Although it contained only ten slices, it felt heavy, substantial in his hand. Like a pork brick. The package specified the product was 'wood-smoked' and 'honey glazed.' *That probably accounts for the price,* Barrett reasoned. *Production costs being passed onto the overworked consumer.* But Barrett was suddenly flush, and anything but overworked. Deciding it was his duty to do his part as a member of the temporary leisure class, he put the pricey bacon in his cart alongside the gourmet cheddar and carried on.

He was trying hard not to think about the past

twenty-four hours. This time yesterday morning, he had still been asleep in Lewis' cells. Since then, he had disobeyed his Archbishop, been adopted by a biker gang, become an accessory after the fact to murder and conducted an illegal funeral and internment on government land. If caught, at bare minimum he was looking at a defrocking and excommunication. Civil authorities, on the other hand, would doubtless demand his sojourn as a guest of the province for at least a decade. But the likelihood of that...

Justice denied, he thought grumpily, wheeling his way down the pasta, condiment and canned meat aisle. He had seen it a dozen times before during his tenure as an investigator: people in authority were held to different standards. Priests, bishops, politicians...

People with friends in low places...

Would the Paladins ever admit to Randy's murder? To the disposal of his body? Barrett figured pigs would fly first. The bikers ('brotherhood of the road,' as Big Mick had it) abided by their 'Code' which, so far as Barrett could tell, was little different from the Mafiosi *omerta*. Nothing short of a full investigation would turn up any clue of his whereabouts and the 'Code' would keep the Paladins mum. Barrett doubted RCMP would invest much time and effort, but you never knew. He was on this train of thought when a hand fell on his shoulder.

"Getting some shopping done, hey? Me, too." Lewis guided his cart up alongside Barrett's. Sniffed. "Early start, huh? Things go that badly with the Archbishop?"

"He's suspended me from duty." Barrett shrugged. "Basically, I collect a paycheck for doing nothing."

"So, you're basically a government worker. Welcome to the club. Although." Lewis stopped his cart and stared straight into Barrett's face. "Truth be told, I've been busy. Randy's disappeared."

"Disappeared? I thought he was in hospital."

Lewis blinked. Barrett cheered inwardly.

"He was." Those two syllables were poured slow as molasses. "Released last night. His mom picked him up. Left him in the car when she ran into the store to get groceries. Came out and he was gone. No sign of him. You haven't seen him, have you?"

"No."

Lewis nodded slowly, turned and began to survey the selection of baked beans.

"See, thing is, Padre... You're kind of in a strange position here. An out-of-work disgraced Vatican investigator who couldn't even keep his nose clean in a fucking backwater like Fulton, British Columbia. You're the last guy to have any, ah, *meaningful* contact with the disappeared. And you seem like the kind of guy to hold a grudge."

"Sergeant, I am the soul of Christian forgiveness. Once I put a man in the hospital, I say an act of contrition and pray heartily for my victim." Barrett grinned. "It's the Catholic thing to do."

"Hm. Now consider this here Heinz bean mix in tomato sauce." Lewis lifted a can from the shelf and brandished it. "Not bad. But I'm more of a Bush's man, myself. How about you?"

"What about me?"

Lewis smiled like an amused dog. "What kind of beans you like?"

"Pinto."

"Diplomatic answer. Shows restraint." Lewis leaned over the handle of his shopping cart and clasped his hands. "I want you to help me."

"Excuse me?"

"Randy! Hello?" Lewis cocked his head. "Ex-Toronto cop? Vatican investigator? You've got some serious professional pedigree and it would be a big help to me. You're not working right now." He spread his hands. "And I'm getting called into Campbell River for these goddam meetings about some damn investigation I'm only peripherally involved with. But I have to show up. Eats a whole day."

"I just drove to Campbell River. It takes forever on these roads."

"I know it. So I'm going to be in and out of town the next few days. What do you say? Poke around for me?"

"Sure."

Not quite as slow as molasses. And Barrett considered it his first slip. But Lewis seemed to take it as reluctance.

"Don't worry. Unofficial. Strictly under the table."

"How much?"

Lewis' eyebrows hoisted. "Ah! Okay…I'll pay you out of our detachment slush fund. A fair rate. Say constable's starting pay?"

Barrett considered. That worked out to around $1,500 per week. "Deal," he said finally.

"Excellent." Lewis poked around in his cart. "I'm going to get in a few hours of fishing. Should be back this evening. Let me know if you find anything."

"I will." Barrett swallowed and narrowed his eyes in what he hoped was an appropriately speculative fashion. "What if he's already dead?"

Lewis became very still. If his gaze were a scale, he was weighing Barrett with his eyes. He drew out the silence again, slow as molasses, before finally answering.

"You better hope he's not, padre. Because if he is, you're the number one suspect."

Barrett actually laughed. "It's a very long list, Sergeant Lewis. From what I can tell, Randy didn't have *any* friends."

"Oh, he had some. As you'll discover. If you do your job."

"I'm very industrious. Habit you pick up in seminary."

"I thought only monks wore habits."

Smart guy, Barrett thought. *I'll have to watch myself.*

Bikers

HOW THE HELL *am I supposed to investigate the disappearance of a man I buried yesterday?*

Barrett sat smoking and drinking coffee on the front porch of the parish house. The town was silent under a grey sky, all the adults who lived on his street at work, all the kids in school. A lone parcel delivery van cruised by, interrupting the silence briefly before vanishing around a corner.

Fulton.

Barrett had been to some pretty godawful places in his time—poverty-stricken, war-torn locales where the church barely hung on by its fingernails, providing the only framework of sanity for believers in a secular hell. Those outposts of human civilization were cradles of misery, but within them always lurked the possibility of redemption—at least of improvement in material circumstances through faith and community. Fulton was different.

The town existed like a bug in amber. A massive stasis hung over it, one held in place by poverty, drug addiction and the tenuous safety net of government assistance. In places like Fulton, things never got worse but they never got better, either. A local election had been held the week after Barrett's arrival and he noted a great many of the lawn signs were recycled from previous years. Like many places in rural BC, political power was shuffled among a small group of wealthy local citizens on the strength of 'promises' that inevitably mutated, under the weight of bureaucratic inertia, into pet infrastructure projects for contractor friends. Citizens, stuck within the town's gravitational pull, surrendered to the despair brought on by stasis.

Barrett heard voices, the ticking of bicycle wheels. That same group of Indian kids in black hoodies who tore around town riding their bikes paused by his hedge. One got off, unzipped his pants, and made ready to take a leak.

"Get out of here!" Barrett bellowed.

The kid's head jerked up. He stuffed himself back into his jeans, jumped on his bike, and tore off with the rest of his crew.

"Go piss somewhere else, you little shit-weasel!" hollered Barrett, shaking a fist.

What a fucking hole this town is!

Barrett checked his watch and decided it was time to switch to beer. He always thought better when drinking beer, and now he was back on the job as a cop.

A 'cop,' he thought, hauling a Sam Adams from the fridge and popping it with his keychain. He wasn't officially on the books (except maybe Lewis' accounting book, under *miscellaneous*). He'd have to watch his step. At the first sign of additional RCMP or Walton, the Conservation officer who shared Lewis' office, he'd have to duck and cover. Twiddle his thumbs and pretend to be doing nothing. But what was more…

I have to come up with some story about my 'investigation.' He took a heavy swig and pondered. *Lewis will probably check the details. It has to sound credible.*

A rumbling shook the street outside. At first Barrett thought it might be a passing steam-roller until the chugging and the thunder became recognizable as Harleys. He stepped to the front door and opened it just as Big Mick and another biker pulled into his driveway with the din of twin B-52s. Mick switched off his hog, dismounted and loped over, stepping inside and pulling Barrett with him.

"You won't fucking *believe* this, padre!" Mick smelled of fear and cannabis. "Somebody dug up Randy. He's fucking *gone*, man!"

———

AND THEN HE WAS, once again, clinging for dear life to a big, hairy biker on the backseat of a Harley as they hurtled at break-neck speed down the Trans-Canada. A camper slowed beside them as they stopped at a red-light junction with a provincial road. The balding, bespectacled retiree driving the thing gawped at the sight of a priest on the back of a hog. Barrett raised his right hand and blessed the man. Then the light changed and they drove on.

Over and around the contours of maintenance roads, into the bush and logging domain they continued until pausing to dismount and hike that same path into the trees. The distance between the road and the burial site was not so huge and forbidding in daylight. Barrett could spot the disinterred grave from afar. Reaching it, he peered down into the black hole framed by leaves and tree rot.

"They left the carpet," he said. But there was no sign of Randy.

"Fuck!" Big Mick was turning around and around, scanning the trees. "Who the *fuck?* I mean, who the *fuck* would do something like this?"

"It's damned indecent," agreed Pappy, standing a little ways off.

As indecent as murdering a man in cold blood and dumping his body in the forest? Barrett wondered. But kept his trap shut.

Mick threw his arms up. "We gotta find him," he pleaded. "Jesus, father. You gotta help us."

It's what I'm being paid to do, Barrett reflected, the presence of his St. Ignatius medal in Randy's front pocket providing no small added incentive.

"So, somebody came right out here." Barrett jammed his hands on his hips and cast around. "Just came right to the spot. Dug him up. Carried him off. For what reason we don't know. But we *do* know that he knew where to look."

"Not necessarily, padre." Pappy stepped forward. "Could have been hunters found it. Could have been a bear dug it up."

"Not a bear," said Big Mick. "A bear would have had himself a snack. Treated himself with a few bites. We'd see blood and skin and shit. Nah. This was a human done this."

Barrett tended to agree. "Obviously someone who knew where we buried him. Whoever he is, he was at the funeral that night."

A ripple of uneasiness passed between them briefly before ribboning off to disappear between the trees.

Pappy and Big Mick let it go, the presence of a traitor among them too weighty a subject to take up among non-Paladins. The energy settled. Then Barrett broke the silence.

"We need to take a look at Randy's life. The people close to him. Obviously, his brother has to be a suspect. Like I said, everyone who was here. Also possible is that someone within your ranks could have just guided someone *else* out here. Does your group have any enemies?"

"Do we?" Big Mick scoffed. "Name them! We got plenty. Probably the Huns are the worst of the lot…"

"But we had that scrape with that Vietnamese gang in Nanaimo last year. Remember?" Pappy evidently did remember and was troubled by it.

"Okay. You guys put together a list and we'll take a look." Barrett gestured back toward town. "But for now, I've got things I have to attend to at the office. Can you guys drop me?"

Big Mick was nodding. "Yeah, sure father. We'll think on it."

"Make one list of Randy's enemies. And another list. *Your* enemies. Enemies of the Paladins. Where those two lists overlap…"

"Gotchya', father. Thing is." Pappy's eyes narrowed as he examined Barrett. "You put that medallion in his pocket. That ties him to you."

"I know."

"Which ties him to us."

Panic surged in Barrett's chest. "Hey. Rest easy." He hid his discomfort behind a breezy smile. "You have the seal of the confessional protecting you. I'm forbidden under pain of eternal damnation from ever revealing that which is entrusted to me by those in need."

"Yeah, well…" Big Mick's jaw firmed and he traced an arc in the soil with the toe of one boot. "We're not Catholic, father."

"Doesn't matter. What is taken to a priest in confidence remains confidential. There are acres of legal precedent for that in this country, dating back to the days before Confederation. Catholicism is a law unto itself."

"So are we," Big Mick said. And laughed. He led them back to the Harleys. A few minutes later, they were on the road for the return trip.

Barrett had them drop him at the liquor store. The same group of Native kids that had stopped to piss on the church hedge earlier that day were arrayed in a semi-circle around the doorway. They all wore black hoodies.

"Hey, *father*," one girl taunted. She was a sallow-faced, mad-eyed little thing, lurking within the shadow of her raised hoodie.

"Hello." Barrett smiled and reached for the door handle.

Some kid spat on his ankle.

Barrett turned slowly in the direction of the spit. Encountered three stone-faced young Native boys, none betraying a single sign of having been the culprit. Barrett struggled with the impulse to fire back with an insult or a punch before deciding the optics weren't good: a grown white man flattening a Native kid half his size and doing it in a clerical collar wouldn't help matters. Barrett decided to leave it at a glare. He stepped inside and asked the cashier for a handi-wipe.

"Little shits, aren't they?" She handed over the container and shook her head. "Man, if my kids acted like that."

Barrett appreciated her parenting philosophy. Bending, he wiped spittle from the hem of his trousers and inside of one shoe.

"They spit on ya'? Fuck them." She stared out the window and shook her head again. "If my kids acted like that. Man."

Barrett deposited the handi-wipe in the trash and ambled down the aisle with the boxed wine. His customary red, the store's cheapest, was in its usual spot on the bottom shelf at the end. Hauling up a box, he turned and saw one of the Indian boys, the one who had tried peeing on the hedge, glaring at him through the window. Barrett gave him the finger.

They were waiting for him when he came outside. The electric door swung wide and Barrett brushed through, hearing a giggle rise behind him. He kept going. A minute passed and then he heard the ticking of bicycle tires coming up from behind. Without looking back, Barrett picked up speed, heading for the parish house.

Then a bicyclist swerved in, forcing Barrett to slow. Suddenly he was surrounded on all sides, hemmed in and unable to move. One kid, the kid who had tried to pee on his hedge, forced his way through the press of handlebars and wheels and bodies to go nose-to-nose with Barrett.

"What did you yell at me as I was riding away?"

Barrett glared and said nothing.

"Fucking white man. You call me a 'shit-weasel'?"

A general murmuring arose. They agreed that 'shit-weasel' sounded truly impolite. Possibly racist.

"Get the fuck out of my way," Barrett snarled. They were the last words out of his mouth before they attacked—a dozen fifteen-year-olds, swarming in on him in a hail of fists and shoes. Barrett covered up against all the hits and kicks as best he could but dropped the wine box. A sneaker found his face, poking his eyeball and hitting his nose such that a massive sneeze built, forcing his eyes shut.

A fist clobbered the back of his head. Another and another. He went down face-first, sprawled flat, arms wrapped over his head, body tensed against blows. He lay there until he heard the ticking of bicycle wheels fade away. And remained a while longer until he rose, groaning under the pain of bruised ribs and a swelling cheek where that kid's shoe had connected. He was busted up good and what was more…

Took my wine, the little bastards!

He stumbled to the parish house and dug out car keys. His shoulder and elbow shrieked as he pulled open the car door. Getting in was a chore but he eventually succeeded, clipping on his seatbelt and starting the ignition. He winced as he spun the wheel, guiding the car around and pointing it in the direction of Lewis' office. He drove the two blocks carefully, as though he might hit a cat, careful to avoid any accidents in his perturbed state.

The office was deserted, the door closed and lights were out. A sign hung in the window.

CALLED OUT OF TOWN
FOR EMERGENCIES, CONTACT RCMP
CAMPBELL RIVER
BACK SOON.

Stolen Valor

"SO HOW MANY of them beat you up?"

"I didn't get *beat up*. They cheated. They swarmed on me."

"Cheated?" Big Mick laughed. "Okay. How many of them beat—Uh, *cheated* and jumped you?"

"I dunno. Around fifteen." Barrett stared glumly through the windshield of Mick's pick-up truck and tested his puffy cheek with a fingertip. Outside, forested hills drifted by as the Trans-Canada unwound beneath them like a spool.

"Fifteen?" Mick gave a low whistle. "What did the cops say?"

"They're not around! Lewis put up a 'gone fishing' sign and fucked off."

"Seen that before." Mick nodded. "Probably out working a poaching case with Walton. Although sometimes, I swear, they just put up that sign and go hunting for a couple of days…"

"Seriously?"

"Sure." Mick thought for a minute, then snapped his

fingers. "I know that little gang of assholes you're talking about. The black hoodie kids. Listen, I could send a couple of the guys out to –"

"No."

"Just scare 'em. Not hurt 'em…"

"No."

"You sure?"

"Yes!" Barrett dug out his cigarettes and jammed one in his mouth. "Beat up a bunch of teenagers? Forget it. No, thanks."

"I'm actually glad." Mick scratched his beard. "Truth is, I kinda admire them."

"What?"

"Most kids these days are real pussies!" Mick complained. "At least these little bastards had the balls to go beat someone up. Most kids nowadays are all prissy about language and wanting them 'safe spaces' to hug pillows and what-not if they get 'triggered' by some shit."

"I'm surprised you know about that."

"Eh, I've got nieces." Mick shrugged. "And a nephew. A real pussy."

"You should be supportive." Barrett smiled ruefully.

"Maybe if he grew a pair." Mick squinted at a passing mileage marker. "Nah. That's not it. Next one."

"This guy lives in the woods? On public land?"

Mick nodded. "Great place to grow. People almost never come through this section of the ALR. It's way too far from any national parks or tourist attractions. Soil is good. You've got canopy cover. Lot of rain. Great place to grow."

A great place to grow. Marijuana was now legal but heavily-regulated in Canada. Product came from government-controlled labs. But if anything this liberalization of drug laws had caused more, not less of a clampdown on small pot farmers. Mick's pal, despite dealing in a lawful substance, was still an outlaw.

At the next mileage marker—little more than a green square topping a single narrow signage pole—Mick guided the truck off the road, across a shallow section of the drainage ditch and onto a level grassland that extended thirty feet to the treeline. Barrett felt the truck jounce over tree roots as they went into the forest cover then, a few seconds later, the sound of a vehicle swishing past on the road they'd just left. Barrett knew they would be invisible to passing traffic. In the wet shadow and musky smell of pine, in the deep presence of ancient soil he reflected this was the sort of land where people could get themselves lost—intentionally or unintentionally—for good.

Like Randy had.

"So, this guy? What was his name?"

"Daryl." Big Mick steered around a huge tangle of blackberry as he spoke. "He's a real piece of work. Thought of him after I started writing those lists you told me to make, our enemies and Randy's. Thing is, Daryl's name is on both."

"Why did he hate Randy?"

"For the same reason everyone did." Barrett heard a bird scream from a nearby tree. "Because Randy was an asshole and a thief. He'd steal shit. Oh yeah! Took a bunch of Daryl's stuff. He—"

Just then Barrett's cell-phone rang. He was surprised he still had coverage this far out in the bush. He tugged it from a pocket.

"Hello?"

"Hello, is this Father Asshole?"

Barrett frowned. "Excuse me?"

"I said is this Father Asshole, the one who likes to beat up Indian kids?"

"WHO IS THIS?"

"You beat up my kid!" The man's voice sounded decidedly First Nations, of that much Barrett was certain. "You jumped him in the street and beat him up. And I'm calling to tell you to watch it."

"Wait a minute. I—"

The man hung up.

"What an asshole!" Barrett snapped his phone shut. "Guys calls me up and accuses me of beating up his kid! Indian guy."

"That's not good." Mick's voice was hesitant. "You don't want them angry at you."

"But I'm the one who got beat up!"

"Doesn't matter."

"This is a really fucked up island." Barrett lit a fresh cigarette. "People treat you like garbage and then you end up getting in trouble for being treated like garbage."

"Yeah. That's about the size of it. That's the way it is here."

"Why the fuck is that?"

"Why knows? Anyway, we were talking about Daryl. Randy came out for a visit and walked off with some of Daryl's weed. Randy was that kind of asshole. You invite him over to get stoned and he ends up walking off with your stash. Daryl told me that's what happened. Before the rift between him and the Paladins."

"Hang on a sec." Barrett fished his phone back out and used the fast dial to ring Scooter. Barrett waited, smoking, through a half-dozen rings before Scooter answered tiredly.

"Hello?"

"Scooter, it's Mike Barrett. Could you do me a favor?

I just got kind of a weird phone call. Sort of threatening. Would you please take a minute and wander over to the parish house? Take a look around and make sure everything is all right?"

"Sure thing, Father." Scooter perked up a bit. "Everything alright with you?"

"So far so good, thanks." Barrett paused as pine branches raked the window of the pick-up. "It's probably nothing. Just a prank in bad taste. But I'd like to be sure. Go over there and check that the place is okay, will you?"

"Will do, father." Scooter hung up.

Barrett saw a break in the trees ahead. They were in deep forest country now, miles from the nearest road and off the electrical grid entirely. The wreckage of old-growth trees, rotted and partially fallen, loomed around moist flatlands like the skeletons of high-rises. The ground was not quite swampy but could get that way quick enough if the rain fell. Tucked behind a tiny grove of tall pines was a fifth-wheel similar to Scooter's. Smoke drifted lazily from a stack on the roof.

"Daryl had some beef with us about a year back. We bought a few pounds of his product. Turned out to be moldy. He only refunded us ten cents on the dollar." Big Mick shrugged as he turned off the ignition. "We didn't make a big thing of it. Let it go. Just resolved not to do business with him again."

"Sounds like you're afraid of him."

"Daryl? Ffft! No way. But, uh. He's always going on about...."

"What?"

"He used to be a Navy SEAL, man."

Barrett laughed. "Right. I wish I had a dime for every ex-Navy SEAL who ends up starting a grow-op on Vancouver Island."

Mick shot him a glance. "You sayin' Daryl's a *liar?*"

"Probably. C'mon. Let's go."

Barrett let himself out of the passenger door, ignoring the tall stand of birch trees nearby and how it reminded him of piano legs. To cover his sudden shortness of breath, he jammed a cigarette between his lips. Then he leaned in and inhaled on the warm breath of his Bic. Because then he could blame it on the smoke.

But the piano legs, the (slightly dulled) sense of panic, the shortness of breath: all these accompanied an uncomfortable memory of childhood, serving to raise the panic he had fought so hard throughout his life to contain. It was the desperately fearful knowledge that—

"Look, father."

A man was approaching, a shotgun in his arms.

—fearful knowledge that he could not escape, like being underneath the piano that night as a toddler when—

"Well, hi!" The man with the shotgun stopped and grinned. "Big Mick, is it?"

Barrett studied the man. He was a chubby, rumpled, balding, bearded hippie-type. Flaccid, fleshy, and physically undisciplined under his cloth windbreaker and workman's cloth cap. The only type of ex-seal he could be, Barrett reckoned, was of the aquatic variety.

"Ho, Daryl!" Big Mick seemed unusually friendly. "How's it goin'?"

The man he'd called Daryl slowed, raising his shotgun, slinging it back across the shoulder, and eyeing Barrett suspiciously. "Who's the priest?" he demanded.

"My name is Barrett." He raised his hands and shielded his rain-soaked eyes. "We're looking for someone who's gone missing. Can we talk to you?"

A brief pause, then: "You already are!"

"Okay." Barrett forced a grin. "We're looking for Randy."

"*Randy?*" Daryl spat. "That pot-lickin' sumbitch? That stash-stealing, demented little asshole freak? What about him?"

"He's gone missing."

"Well, halle-fuckin'-lujah!"

"You don't know anything about it?"

"Know anything about it? No. Am I overjoyed about it? Hell, yes! Fuck that little fucker."

"So he wasn't exactly a friend?"

"Fuck no!"

Barrett was beginning to get the picture. "So he was a hostile? I'd expect you'd know."

"Damn right I would!"

"Big Mick here says you were a Navy SEAL."

"Sure was."

"Uh-huh. When were you decommissioned?"

"Oh." The man smiled. That kind of question was easy. "Two years ago, December."

"I see. And where was your last roto?"

Daryl squinted. Barrett could see the wheels turning. *Roto, he's thinking. Short for…*

"Oh, my last rotation? Through Iraq." Daryl smiled. "Sorry padre, but you Canadians have a different way of putting things from what I'm used to."

"Sure." Barrett recognized a practiced liar and smiled. "Well, I can see you're the real deal. Let me shake your hand. It's an honor to meet a real US Navy SEAL, yessir."

Daryl, lips pursed, moved forward and gave a stiff nod, as if to say *'okay, I forgive you.'* He shook.

"So, Randy." Barrett jammed his hands on his hips. "You have some trouble with him?"

"Sure did." Daryl spat. "Sumbitch. Last summer. Said he needed a place to stay. Him and his dad weren't getting along. So I said sure. Come stay here with me. So Randy did. Pot-lickin' sumbitch."

"How long did he stay?"

"Only about two weeks." Daryl spat and Barrett realized he was dipping chewing tobacco. A great wad of it trembled in his lower lip as he spoke. "After two weeks, I figured out that he was skimming some of the harvest. Little bit each day. When he went out for a walk, I searched his luggage and found a big old bag of the stuff. Was waiting with the shotgun when he returned. Told the sumbitch to get and ain't seen him since."

Barrett studied Daryl carefully, giving him the same blank, measuring glance Lewis had given him. He could not, for the life of him, imagine that Daryl was lying about this. Practiced liar though he may be, he was not lying about this.

"Randy's missing, Daryl." Big Mick's tone was terminal.

"So you said." Daryl spit. "He ain't been here. Don't know where he is. Don't care. And fuck him."

Barrett believed him.

"So?" Big Mick raised his eyebrows.

Barrett shrugged.

They turned to go.

"Hey, Daryl?"

"Yes, father?" The fat, dumpy man turned back looking tired, wasted out. As if Barrett had interrupted him on his way to a nap. Or a shot of whatever he was hooked on these days.

"Who was your swim buddy?"

Daryl thought for a minute. "Dave Edwards."

"And your BUDs class number?"

A longer thought.

"Ah, 586?"

Barrett nodded. By his calculations, BUDs class 586 would acquaint aspiring SEALs with the intricacies of diving, explosives, and covert assassination sometime around 2030 AD or so.

"Pleasure meeting you, sir."

"And you, father."

———

IT WAS a leisurely drive home back through the forest. Big Mick called a pause after 45 minutes and they dismounted to piss, drink beer, and share a joint Mick explained was some exotic form of Hawaiian brain-fuck ganja. They squatted inside the tree-line just off of the highway, watching vehicles sweep past, passing the joint back and forth and mellowing in the silence until Big Mick spoke.

"So. What do you think of Daryl, father?"

"He's a total bullshit artist. He's no SEAL."

"Oh, yeah?"

"Yeah." Barrett accepted the joint and sucked on it lightly twice. "He hesitated before he told me the name of his swim buddy, which is totally fundamental to SEAL training lore. And his BUDs class number was all out-of-whack. No. He's making everything up."

"And Randy?"

"He doesn't know shit about Randy. I know it."

Big Mick nodded sadly. They got back into the truck and drove the last 45 minutes into town. The sun was setting as they cruised onto the main drag. The drop in temperature was immediate and noticeable, causing

Barrett to shiver. Big Mick steered in the direction of the church. A white cube was parked at the curb out front. It took Barrett a moment to recognizing it as an ambulance.

"Expecting company, father?"

Barrett got out and sprinted around back. Someone had spray-painted something across the church wall. Barrett caught individual letters but the message itself blurred past as Barrett sprinted around the building and made for the paramedics kneeling halfway between the church and Scooter's RV, tending to something on the ground.

"What the hell?" Barrett skidded to a stop.

"Hey, father." Scooter's face was a welter of blood and bruises. Two paramedics were splinting his arm. "I went and looked in on the church like you asked…"

"WHO DID THIS?" Barrett was furious—killing mad. *I bet it's those Indian kids!* He fought a spasm of rage. Scooter was just about the nicest, most peaceful guy Barrett had ever met in his life. There was *no* justi-fication…

"I checked the place several times. Came around the corner about an hour ago and saw somebody in a black hoodie spray-painting the church wall. When I yelled at him to stop, he took out one of those clubs. You know the kind that fold up like a telescope?"

"ASP baton, father," said one of the paramedics. He pointed at Scooter's elbow. "Broke his arm."

Barrett gritted his teeth and did his best to calm the rage erupting within him.

"I ran." Scooter coughed. Barrett could see he was holding back tears. "Tried to get to my trailer to call the cops but he. They. I don't know. Jumped me. And… Well, fuck 'em. Here I am."

"It's *okay,* Scooter. It's okay. You done good. Just get better, okay?"

"We're going to run him up to the hospital," said the paramedic. "We'll keep him overnight for observation."

"I'm sorry, father..." Scooter's voice was a weak croak. The tears began. "I—"

"Scooter, relax." Barrett laid his hand over Scooter's as the paramedics secured the stretcher rail. Barrett followed them to the street where they loaded him into the ambulance. They promised to bring back Scooter in the morning. Barrett thanked them then stood, watching solemnly alongside Big Mick as they drove away.

"Sorry, father," muttered Big Mick. "Sure you don't want me to send some guys after those kids?" he asked, waving a hand toward the graffiti on the church wall. Barrett turned and read it in its entirety for the first time.

THE ONLY GOOD PRIEST IS A DEAD PRIEST

Devil's Advocate

"O...KAY." Ann Fletcher, Esquire, sighed and pushed her eyeglasses up into her salt-and-pepper bangs, peering across her desk at Barrett with that admixture of friendliness and pity he had come to expect from women his own age. It was a vaguely interrogative expression—one that seemed to ask how somebody as obviously masculine and whole as Barrett could have ended up a sexless celibate in a monkey suit. So, he was not entirely surprised when she asked: "How long have you been a priest?"

"Fifteen years."

"Any regrets?" she smiled.

"Nope." Barrett looked out the window and pined for a cigarette.

"Never wanted a family? Kids? A...woman?"

Barrett gave a convincing if slightly annoyed smile and his canned answer to such intrusive female probing. "A priestly vocation carries its own rewards."

"Cagey one, aren't you? That's okay. I've dealt with male clients who have—well, let's call them 'insecurities' before." She gave a husky chuckle. "It's not easy coming to a woman for help, I know."

"I'll let you know. The moment I get some."

She inhaled—the sort of inhale that signals self-control, restraint, an 'I'm-too-polite-to-sigh' attitude. Barrett knew he had just registered on her scale of value as 'rude.' And although it was not an adjective he often applied to women, he privately considered Ann Fletcher, Esquire, an asshole.

But an expensive one, he thought, glancing at his watch. He was paying for her time.

"So." She refocused attention on her notepad. "You were attacked on the date in question by a gang of First Nations youth on bicycles. Because police services were unavailable—I take it Gavin was out on one of his hunting trips—the matter remains unaddressed. And then there was the graffiti on the church and the attack on your sexton, Scooter is it? Is that his given name?"

"No. It's Charles Andrew Hamilton."

"…attack on Mr. Hamilton. And you're convinced it's the same group?"

Barrett smacked his palm with a fist. "Scooter was attacked by one or more people in black hoodies. Those bike kids have a grudge against me and they wear the same outfit. Plus the graffiti on the church. Seems pretty straightforward to me."

Again, the patient inhale. "Alright. So you want to go RJ?"

"I'm sorry?"

"Restorative Justice. That's where we sit down with the boys and a representative of the tribe and hash it out. It's a non-judicial proceeding. Fairly standard for first offenders."

"I doubt these kids are first offenders."

"But they *are* youth. Which means…May I be frank? It means the criminal justice system is going to give them a bye." Ann Fletcher, Esquire, tossed a fatalistic shrug. "Bottom line? Kids can more or less do whatever they want to whomever they want these days and the courts aren't going to do anything about it."

"That's bullshit."

"That's democracy."

Barrett gritted his teeth, fighting down frustration.

"Another thing, too." She adopted a gentler tone. Barrett steeled himself for more bad news. "If you go to the tribe with this—even just for an RJ hearing—without conclusive evidence that their youth are to blame, you're opening yourself to a lawsuit." She held up a hand. "Right or wrong, that's how justice rolls these days. And the tribes have deep pockets, both their own and what they cull from government grants to facilitate 'reconciliation.' The way I see this going is: we sit down, you state your case, the kids claim they're innocent, and the chief ends the meeting by saying he needs to consult with the tribe's attorney. Next thing you know, boom. Lawsuit against the Catholic Church."

Barrett simmered.

"Look, residential schools loom large in the public mind these days, to say nothing of litigation. My advice?" She pushed her notepad aside. "Suck it up. Wait for Lewis to come back. Let him investigate before you do anything else."

Barrett checked his watch. A half-hour in her office meant he had burned $150. Time to cut his losses.

"Okay." He rose. "Thank you. I'll need some time to think about this."

"Of course." She stood and extended a hand. As they shook, she added: "I know it's hard for you guys to put your pride aside. You want revenge, but that kind of impulse is what's gotten us into the mess we're in."

Barrett suppressed a shudder. For Ann Fletcher, Esquire, the future was undoubtedly female.

———

HE KEPT an eye peeled for Indian kids on his stopover at the liquor store but there was no sign of them. *Laying low,* he figured, marching up to the counter with a gallon of cheap Chianti. He intended to make pasta for lunch. And perhaps dinner, as well. The cashier noted his nervous glances at the front window.

"You looking for them kids?"

"Yeah."

"Some old fat guy in a green baseball cap showed up. Native. Didn't hear what he said, but he talked to them real calmly for about ten seconds. Then they all mounted up and followed him, all quiet-like." She shook her head. "Damndest thing I ever seen. Wish my kids acted like that. Man."

Barrett wondered about it as he walked home. Likely they had done something on the rez for which were being called to answer, the old fat guy in the green ballcap probably someone's uncle or father. Barrett's dealing with First Nations had been fairly limited. There were a few who came to Sunday services but not with sufficient regularity for him to get to know.

And I won't now, he thought.

He was almost level with the church before realizing the jumble of boxes and the rear of the station wagon poking out into the street were from his own driveway. Frowning, he stepped around an exercise contraption blocking the sidewalk, one of those that induces its victim into making cross-country ski movements, and into a sea of white moving boxes. A large, squat figure was dawdling down the driveway in Barrett's direction from the parish house, carrying some type of old-fashioned mixing machine. It reminded Barrett of the sort of thing they once made milkshakes in. The man carrying it was probably around fifty-five or so, as wide as he was tall, balding and wearing a dazed smirk. The clerical collar told Barrett what he had begun to suspect. Here was his replacement.

"Hello." The man's voice was soft, his tone, bland. He did not so much meet Barrett's gaze as glance in his direction before setting the mixing machine down amongst a jumble of stuff in the station wagon's rear. Then he pulled a handkerchief from his pocket, wiped his hands, re-folded it carefully, replaced it in his pocket and looked up to adjust his glasses and consider Barrett.

"You'd be Barrett." The man's voice was almost inaudible. Barrett had to adjust his stance and cock his head to catch the words. "I'm Father Dolan. Come in. I was just making lunch."

"I see you've made yourself at home," said Barrett drily. The swipe didn't seem to register with Dolan, who had turned back to the station wagon to examine the heaps of stuff in there. Barrett peered in and was almost convinced that, among the pair of television sets, the chest of drawers laid on its side, the heaped piles of clothing and boxes of books were also stacks of newspaper—tied bundles of paper editions, kept in storage for what reason he could only guess. Dolan removed a golf bag from amongst the strewn debris and shouldered it, ambling back up the driveway in the same distracted dither with which he had approached. Barrett hurried to join him.

"So, you got the key from—?"

"There's a nice stash of pasta in the kitchen," interrupted Dolan. He turned to regard Barrett with his complete attention for the first time, his gaze moist and strangely accusatory. "I put on a pot of spaghetti. Nice big pot. I'm hungry."

"I...see." Barrett frowned. So the little asshole had let himself in and just raided the pantry. "Archbishop Crowe says you've worked in the parish before."

Dolan said nothing. They approached the side door and walked into the kitchen. Boxes and bags crammed with stuff crowded every available surface. Barrett wondered at the change in normal lighting until realizing that even the windowsills were piled with stuff (mostly tall, leaning stacks of paperback books). His good, copper-bottom pot belched a volcano of steam from the stove.

"U-Haul left half-an-hour ago." Dolan set the golf bag in a corner alongside the most impressive collection of mops and brooms this side of a janitorial closet Barrett had ever seen. "They were a couple of nice girls, the moving company sent. Very efficient. I gave them the box of wine in the cupboard as a tip, I hope that was okay. No need for that much wine around here. Unless you were...?"

But by then Barrett had cracked open the Chianti and seized his coffee mug from the dish drainer. *This guy,* he thought, pouring himself a mugful, *is going to wind up dead if he isn't careful.*

He downed the mug in one long swallow.

Dolan was staring at him again with that watery, accusatory stare. "You like wine?" he asked. And then answered his own question. "Yes, I can see that. I can see you like wine. That's obvious."

"You got the key from Archbishop Crowe, I would imagine?"

"I received a call," muttered Dolan in his irritating, distracted, whispery way, "from Archbishop Crowe. Always such a pleasure to hear from him. He's such a nice man. Don't you think? I think so. I think he's a truly nice man. Anyway, I received a call. From Archbishop Crowe."

Barrett downed a second mug of Chianti and struggled not to punch Dolan square in the mouth.

"Archbishop Crowe asked me to come up. Seems I'm to take over. From you. Which, may I be frank? Which, frankly, is the way it probably *should* have been to begin with. I was already *here*. I had already moved *in*."

Barrett glanced at a tower of shoeboxes occupying the corner. "You didn't put any of this shit in my room, did you?"

"Oh, don't worry. Your stuff is all perfectly safe. I put it all in the garage."

"You *what?*"

"Well." Dolan straightened over the stove, a dripping fork in one hand. "I didn't want it damaged. I have a lot of personal effects to store and needed the space."

Barrett put the mug down with a decisive *click*. "Look. Father Dolan. I appreciate your—"

"Hand me that can of spaghetti sauce?"

"No. I'm talking. I—"

"I'm asking for your help here."

"Father Dolan, I—"

Dolan abruptly put down the fork, stepped away from the boiling pot, and pulled a cell-phone from his pocket. He walked from the room with it, studying his text messages as he went.

Barrett blinked.

Son-of-a-bitch!

Pouring himself another mug of wine, he stepped out to the garage. Sure enough, his belongings, crammed into a dozen boxes, were piled alongside the headboard and box-spring of his bed. His mattress stood on its side against the wall. A scatter of his table-top belongings—keys, eyeglasses, spare packs of cigarettes—were strewn on the workbench.

Bastard!

Barrett crossed back into the kitchen, closing the door behind him. He decided he might as well take a look and see what Dolan had done with the rest of the place. There was nothing in the entrance hall aside from more boxes. He walked into the living room. And felt his insides turn to liquid.

A baby-grand piano sat in the middle of the floor.

Barrett stumbled, reaching out with one hand for the wall, his head spinning. Suddenly he was a child *(a kid)* again, staring out through people's *(piano)* legs toward the lit doorway through which he *(it)* would come and then the…

Next thing he knew, he was grappling his ringing cell-phone from a pocket.

"Hello?"

"Padre, it's Lewis. I need you down at the detachment now. Right now."

"Jesus, Lewis where have you—"

"Dammit, we don't have time for that. Get down here. *Now.*" The Mountie hung up.

The Huns

FOR A MOMENT, as he reached for the door handle of the RCMP detachment, Barrett thought the throbbing and shuddering in his skull was just the usual hangover. But as the din grew, forcing him to squint, he recognized, without even turning around, the full-throated roar of Harley Davidsons. He figured it must be the Paladins out for a good time. Setting his jaw, he turned the handle and let himself in.

Lewis was waiting, seated on the edge of his desk. Walton, the Conservation Officer, a straw-haired man who seemed a prematurely old thirty, was doing paperwork on his office computer.

"Adam, this is him." Lewis narrowed his eyes. "That priest you kept an eye on for me overnight. The one who put Randy in hospital."

Walton raised his head slowly. "Oh. Yeah." He put down his pen. "Hope you're not planning to make a habit of that, father. You should really stick to giving sermons. Leave the law enforcement to us."

"I can't even give sermons anymore." Barrett grabbed a chair from in front of Lewis' desk and twisted it around to face them both. "My replacement arrived," he said, taking a seat.

"Father Dolan?" Lewis glanced at Walton, who sighed.

"Yeah." Barrett smirked. "You know him?"

Walton brayed laughter.

"He frequently calls the detachment." Lewis spoke tightly. "If I didn't know better, I'd say he's a badge bunny. But no. He's just a very nervous, lonely individual who I made the mistake of giving my off-duty cell number to, figuring we'd be in touch maybe if somebody died in a traffic accident or there was a murder or something. Not every night. Twice, three times per night. He sure likes to talk on the telephone does our Father Dolan."

"And he's got a lot of junk, too!" Walton pitched a pencil point-first into his pencil cup. "Hoarder. Real head-case."

"I don't like his piano," murmured Barrett.

"Sorry, what was that?" Lewis was leaning forward, curious.

"Piano." Barrett cleared his throat. "I don't…like his piano. It takes up a lot of room."

"Ah."

Walton and Lewis both seemed to be staring at him. It gave Barrett a distinctly uncomfortable feeling.

"So." Lewis smiled and smoothed his slacks. Smiled wider. "Your replacement is here. You have time on your hands and—"

The din of bikes rose. All of them turned to the window.

"Fuck," said Walton. "It's the Huns."

"Wait." Barrett groped for cigarettes. "I thought the Paladins were our pet bikers."

"They *are,*" Walton grunted. "They're our Riki-Tiki-Tavi. The Huns? They're the cobras."

"That's encouraging." Barrett lit a cigarette despite Lewis' withering glare. "Why are they here in force? Unless it's to—"

The long silence answered him.

Walton stood and unlocked a steel cupboard against the back wall. "Reckon we should break out the hardware, what do you think, Gavin?"

"Sounds like a *fine* idea." Lewis sighed and put down his coffee cup, reached out and accepted the gun-belt Walton proffered. "How's your investigation coming, padre? Any new leads? Don't worry. Adam's aware of our little arrangement and he'll stay mum. Won't you, Adam?"

"Mum about what, exactly, Gavin?"

"See what I mean?" Lewis buckled the belt into place and retrieved his duty-issue Smith & Wesson 5946 from a drawer. "What have you found out?"

Barrett drew a deep breath and let his eyes fall to the floor, figuring out a way to thread as much truth as possible into the tapestry of lies he was about to spin. "Nothing from the store where he was grabbed. I talked to a few witnesses—shoppers, not employees…"

"How'd you track them down?" Walton sounded impressed.

"By chance, actually." Barrett managed a weary smile. "Overheard two people talking about it at the café next door."

"Get their names?" Lewis glanced up from checking the load on his S&W.

"Nah. Anyway, all I got from them was Randy was in

the car, they heard some yelling and then he was gone. I'm working up one lead…"

"Yeah?"

"It's possible he may have gone into the forest." Barrett cautioned himself to take it slow here. He gave an off-handed shrug. "I don't really have much by way of evidence. I'm sort of playing a hunch against a guess, but…"

"Why the forest?" Lewis was interested. "What information do you have?"

"Caught a glimpse of a photo taken from one of those motion detector trail cams. Some guy at the sporting goods store was showing them to a friend…"

"Who?"

"Don't know. There was a blurred image. When I caught sight of it, I thought…Well, I thought it might have been Randy."

Barrett let that drop and fell silent.

"That's it?" Lewis sounded on the verge of upset.

Barrett met his gaze. "And I have one CI."

"Okay." That mollified him. "Can you tell me who—?"

"No."

"Okay." Lewis dropped it. Keeping confidential informants confidential was a typical courtesy between investigators and Barrett knew it. Claiming the CI gave him leverage—a way for him to drop misleading 'facts' into his progress reports. It was also a safe way to weave Big Mick and the Paladins into whatever narrative he might need to spin.

"Looks like the Huns have rolled up on the Junction." Walton, hands on his hips, was still covering the window. "I count…twenty hogs."

"Great." Lewis sighed and went to stand beside him. "We'll have keep an eye on that…"

"There's one more thing," said Barrett. "I got assaulted."

Lewis turned, a smirk on his face. "You got assaulted? By who?"

"That would be 'by *whom*'," corrected Walton with a chuckle.

"Oh, fuck off. Grammar Nazi." Lewis shook his head. "Who beat you up, padre?"

"You know that gang of Indian kids in black hoodies who ride around town on bikes?"

"The rez rats? Jesus, Padre." Lewis threw up his hands. "They're all, like, fourteen years-old!"

"Sure. But, in packs? Kids can be dangerous."

Lewis and Walton exploded in laughter. Barrett endured it silently and was set to continue his story when Lewis raised his hand.

"I did hear something about it, honestly." He winked. "Don't worry, padre. It's under control."

"Are you going to arrest—"

"I said it's under control. Now relax." Lewis turned his attention back to the street. "Go talk to your CI and see what else you can dig up on Randy. I'll be in touch."

'Dig up' on Randy? Barrett savored the irony of that. It was entirely too rich not to. He sighed, rose, and began shuffling for the door.

"Oh, hey. Padre." Walton stepped back to his desk. "Someone dropped this off for you."

The CO extended a package—one of those brown packing envelopes with the bubble-wrapped interior, about six inches by four. Barrett took it and glanced at the front. Someone had written *'FATHER BARRETT'* in block capitals. He tucked it under his arm and turned to go.

"Next time have your mail delivered at the church," Lewis grumbled. "We're not the goddam Canada Post."

Barrett suppressed his response and moved out onto the sidewalk.

The temperature had dropped a few degrees and it looked like a storm might be blowing in from over the mountains. Barrett turned the collar of his tweed jacket against the cold. Coming from across the street, drifting through the open door of the Junction, he could hear laughter and the inevitable Eighties radio rock on the jukebox. He hesitated before angling his steps that way. According to the complex mental heraldry of his alcoholism, going to a bar during daylight hours signified a certain level of failure. Or surrender. Unless he had recently been through a crisis, which…

Fuck it, I'll drop in and have a beer.

The two big goons in the jean vests—a couple of full-patch hoodlums by the look of them—just so happened to be sipping their beers on either side of the entrance when he walked in. They paused, foreheads wrinkling in puzzlement as the middle-aged man in the priest collar ambled up.

"Howdy, fellas," he said with a smile, and ghosted inside.

The Huns crowded the interior of the cozy bar. At the pool-table, four guys eyed up the balls beneath posters of James Dean and Elvis. Another six occupied the bar. The remainder were scattered around, occupying booths and tables, lounging on the jukebox or working the pinball machine. As Barrett found himself a stool, he dug out his cigarettes and placed the envelope on the bar. The barkeep, the same bearded blond guy as the other night, came up and set down a full pint of Guinness in front of the priest, unasked.

"Good to see you here, father," the kid said, voice tight. "These boys are rowdy."

"You okay?" Barrett glanced around and decided the kid probably was right to feel nervous. Barrett, his police background aside, knew his priestly status bought him a certain immunity from violence. But even a priest wouldn't be immune if things turned ugly here all of a sudden.

"I'm okay, just…" The kid stalled for time by rear-ranging some beer glasses on the counter top.

"Take it easy, son." Barrett sipped his beer. "Cops are keeping an eye peeled across the street, they won't let anything go off—"

"HEY, KID! GIMME ANOTHER LAGER!"

Barrett glanced at the man who had cried out. He was a bald, tanned dude with two big diamond ear-rings and a ring threaded through his wide, flat nose like a bull. He glared at Barrett and seemed on the point of challenging him. Barrett swallowed his pride and showed submission by looking away first. He studied the neon beer sign above the bar, yawning, sipping his Guinness and then taking up the package Walton had handed him.

When had envelopes gotten so fucking elaborate? Barrett found the skin of the thing tear-resistant owing to the bubble wrap inside so had to content himself by laboriously peeling back the self-sealing flap. He spread the lips of the package and upended it. And stopped breathing the moment his St. Ignatius medal tumbled onto the bar before him. The world faded out and suddenly Barrett could hear only numb silence and the sound of his heart pounding in his ear drums.

As casually as he could, he scooped it up and

dropped it into a pocket. Barrett heard the approaching roar of Harleys on the street outside. And caught sight of Jackie ducking out the back door.

Invasion

JACKIE?

Barrett half-rose.

The din of Harleys reached a crescendo before dying off one motor at a time outside the bar. The fact that another batch of bikes had pulled up to the Junction was not lost on the assembled Huns, who variously sat back from their tables, turned from the juke to face the door or repositioned themselves on bar-stools so each had one boot on the floor.

There was going to be trouble.

Barrett drained his beer quickly and stood. He planned to make a break for the back door or, failing that, the washroom. But his passage across the empty dance-floor caught the attention of several Huns. Just then the door burst open and Big Mick strode in at the head of a crowd of Paladins.

"Well, how the fuck do you like this, huh?" He swaggered to the middle of the dance floor and paused, arms crossed. "Buncha' fuckin' *Huns* in our bar. Somebody better call the exterminator."

Pappy, Jack, and the other Paladins guffawed loudly at this. But the bald Hun, the one with the nose-ring, slammed down his beer and stalked over to stand toe-to-toe with Pappy. The fat, bearded biker and the sinewy, brown bald biker glared at each other as their respective honchos closed in all around them. This had the unplanned effect of pushing Barrett into Big Mick's line of sight.

"Hey, father! Enjoying a nice cold beer, eh? You wanna watch me pound this nose-ring motherfucker? This no good, sheep-fucking, pedophile *bitch*."

"*THE FUCK!*" the bald Hun exploded. "What the fuck are you on about, Mick? Where the fuck you get off slinging names like that around?"

"Yeah," said Barrett. "Particularly since, you know, you called him a pedo and he isn't even a priest…"

The joke fell completely flat. Mick and the bald Hun shot Barrett a glance before getting back down to cases.

"You better explain yourself, Mick! You got five seconds before my boys turn yours inside out."

"You know goddam well what I'm talking about, Hunter. Now where's Jackie?"

Oh, fuck. Barrett started trying to walk backwards out of the crowd, much as he had tried sneaking into movies as a kid. Hunter, meanwhile, looked suddenly clueless.

"Excuse me? Who?" Hunter sounded genuinely puzzled. "Mick, I don't know anybody named Jackie." He turned to his guys. "Anybody here know a Jackie?"

The assembled Huns gaped at each other and shrugged.

"*BULLSHIT!*" Big Mick stomped a thunderous boot. "If you had any idea what that girl had been through. Tell 'em, father!"

"Uh…" Barrett paused his escape and flashed a watery smile. "You see, Jackie is Mick's little girl. And she recently suffered a…tragedy." *Jesus, could I sound any less convincing?* Barrett hovered there on his toes, waiting to either push off or re-enter the fray. Above the hubbub of voices, his cop's ear, attuned even after all this time, detected the stealthy *snick* of the door opening. A glance confirmed what he had suspected: Lewis and Walton had just walked in. Barrett crossed himself and gave hasty thanks.

"That's *right*," Mick snarled. "My little girl's been through a tragedy, like the father here says. I know she's been hangin' out with one of your boys, Hunter. And you better tell me which one or else—"

"Or else *what?*"

Lewis' gravelly voice cut through the drama and sliced into the dance floor between Big Mick and Hunter the Hun like a one-ton cleaver. The crowd of bikers parted at the lawman's approach. Barrett had to hand it to the old-timer. He was twice the age of most of the assembled hoods, but he carried himself like a lion on the hunt, the determined glint in his eye burning like the fire of justice itself.

"This establishment is hereby closed by law enforcement and will be cleared *at once* in the interest of public order!" Lewis wheeled on Hunter. "You and your boys will saddle up and leave Fulton. In the name of the Law, in the name of the Crown. Do it now, or I will not be held responsible for what happens next."

CLACK!

The crowd turned to see Walton standing atop the bar, freshly-pumped shotgun held at port-arms as he scanned the crowd.

Lewis smiled softly. "Run along now, Hunter."

Nostrils flared, eyes wide and staring, Hunter turned away. Barrett was unsettled by the slowness of the move, the hypnotically deliberate nature of it. Hunter was 'running along' with the insouciant slowness of an outsize bear cub you just caught rooting through your dumpster on a hot Saturday afternoon. You know he's leaving, you don't like that he's taking his time. So you just sort of stand there and hope for the best. Which is what Lewis was apparently doing when Hunter swung back around and sucker-punched Big Mick. Walton's shotgun blew a hole in the roof tiles and all hell broke loose.

A hundred fists, a blur of bodies in denim and leather—Barrett raised his arms against the storm. A distant twinkling in his corner of his eye materialized into a swung belt-buckle that he narrowly ducked. Then Lewis was beside him.

"C'mon, padre! You're up!"

Barrett groaned and moved in beside Lewis riot-squad style, taking up a position at the Mountie's shoulder and covering Lewis' right. Lewis would, in turn, be covering their combined left. With the duty shared, their offensive power doubled. Or such was the theory. Barrett had only been deployed to riot squad once and that had been during a football game back in the days when a minor gathering of twelve or more constituted a 'riot.' They had spent three hours hunkered in a dressing room, watching the game on closed circuit TV until it was time to go home.

A hurled mug exploded into fragments on a nearby wall. Barrett intercepted a fist coming toward him, blocked and then body-checked a moustachioed Hun out of his way. Lewis had yanked out his hand-taser and was applying the juice to a fat, bald fucker who hollered and jiggled where he froze, rooted to the dance floor.

Walton, meanwhile, was re-loading his pump-action with what resembled buckshot cartridges. Barrett managed to fight his way forward through the thinning crowd of bikers. A few had retreated altogether while a handful spasmed where they lay, tasered. One biker lunged to grab Lewis, only to be thrown against the wall in a hurl of rock-shot. From the bar Walton grinned and threw Barrett a thumb's up.

The last few scattered Huns and Paladins were bunching into groups of two and threes, backing away from each other, hollering and gesturing. Lewis had turned, his last biker felled and twitching at his feet while Barrett, gasping and light-headed from the exertion, teetered on his heels. He grasped the back of a chair to stay upright. That's when he noticed Big Mick. He and Hunter were tangled up in a kind of half-assed wrestler's clinch, dancing around while firing random punches at each other. Lewis stowed his taser unit, dipped his hand into his other pocket and produced a small black cylinder. He flicked his fist and a foot of titanium sprang from the grip of the ASP baton. Lewis swung and Hunter collapsed, howling, grasping his knee in both hands. Barrett restrained Big Mick as he lunged in to finish Hunter.

"Enough," Barrett rasped. "Outside. Now. *Right* now."

He and Lewis dragged the Paladins' president out into the empty parking lot behind the Junction. Big Mick came docilely enough, struggling only when the thunder of the Huns' bikes rose from around front. Lewis and Barrett stopped and planted him under a broken streetlamp in the paved quarter-acre from which grass sprouted through cracks in the cement.

"Mick. What the hell was that?" Barrett fought to

keep his inner volcano under control. "You come to me for help and then you behave like *that* in public?"

"I'm sorry, father!" Mick snatched his arm out of Barrett's grasp but shook his head contritely. "But Jackie's gone missing."

"How long she been gone, Mick?" Lewis was all business. "Tell us what you know and Walton and I will get right to work. But you have to be honest with us about anything…questionable, alright?"

"I'm not gonna hide nuthin'!"

"Good! So start telling us what you know." This time when Barrett put his hand on Mick's shoulder, the biker didn't shake it off. "When did you notice she was missing?" At this, Mick forced himself to remain still and take a few deep breaths. Barrett admired the man's self-control.

"It was yesterday evening. I stopped by her room. She wasn't there." Mick shrugged. "Jackie, she has a routine, like. After dinner she goes to her room and watches movies on her laptop. One of the brothers stopped by with a package for her from the club PO box. Went up to her room to deliver it and, boom. No Jackie."

"She never goes out?" Lewis sounded skeptical. "Doesn't meet friends for coffee or Tupperware parties or whatever the fuck it is girls get up to these days?"

"Jackie, she prefers guys. Doesn't like other girls. She's a guy's girl. Knows how to pull a transmission apart. Loves to hunt. Throw a football around. But when she wants to, she can go all heels and make-up and knows how to play the role. Ya' know?"

"So she's a pretty complex little girl then," Lewis said sympathetically, prompting Big Mick to smile.

"Yeah." He chuckled. "Thing is. She's got secrets."

"So…why did you think she'd be with the Huns?" Barrett managed to ask this without any indication of what he had seen earlier crossing his face.

"Like I said." When Big Mick's eyes met Barrett's, they were troubled. "Because she has secrets, padre. And I don't know what they are."

———

SECRETS.

Half of life's problems, Barrett reflected as he walked home, pausing occasionally to dab at his bruised jaw with a handkerchief, could be traced back to secrets. The need for silence, drama, for cloak-and-dagger duplicity accounted for more than its fair share of the world's nonsense. And women seemed to have the corner on the market. It was, Barrett reflected, pausing to duck into the liquor store, as if secrets were some sort of tool necessary to operate the female psyche. And a young, good-looking creature like Jackie would have a grab-bag to choose from, even if dating a guy from the enemy motor cycle club seemed an unlikely move for the kid of the local chapter president.

Oh, well, Barrett reflected, hauling a fresh box of wine to the cash register, *kids always find some way to rebel…* The woman behind the counter rung up his purchase.

"Guy was in here looking for you earlier," she told him. "Older Native guy. Wearing a green ball-cap."

"Same one who dealt with the kids here?" Barrett asked, remembering.

"Yeah. Came in, asked if I had seen you. Says he needs to talk to you."

"I'm easy to find. Just look for the building with the

big 'T' on the roof." Barrett shrugged, picked up his wine and receipt and began the final stretch back to the parish house.

He felt in his pocket for the St. Ignatius medal. With its sudden appearance, his problems had risen to three, but none more pressing than to discover who was on to him. The medal, like the graffiti, was a warning. Someone was determined to trespass into his private affairs. Which immediately made him think of Father Dolan. Barrett wondered if every conceivable square foot of the house was now occupied with his replacement's bric-a-brac. Whatever else he may be intending to do, Barrett reflected, eventually moving out didn't seem to be part of Dolan's plan.

Barrett turned the corner, not surprised to see a jumble of items littering the end of his driveway. It was only when Barrett drew level with the rear of Dolan's station wagon that he realized the items weren't Dolan's, but his own.

Moving Day

"YOU THREW ALL my shit out onto the curb?"

"My. You're so *angry*, Father Barrett. You really *should...*"

"You threw all my shit out onto the curb?"

"...*see* someone about it. It's not healthy. You know anger can actually shorten a person's life?"

"Yes, Father Dolan, I can very easily imagine how the anger I'm feeling right now could shorten someone's life. Very easily."

Dolan, if he took Barrett's meaning, gave no sign. He was bent over a golf ball, sighting along the shaft of his putter, preparing to putt it into a high-ball glass. The glass lay on its side a short distance away down the narrow passageway between stacks of boxes piled to the parish house ceiling. The house was now so packed with Dolan's crap that Barrett was no longer sure where one room ended and another began.

"It was, simply, the best solution I could think of at the time. Oh, bugger." Dolan's putt went wide. The ball skittered across carpet and thunked onto the wood of the living room floor, where it kept rolling. Dolan followed. "It came down, Father Barrett, to the plain and simple fact that there wasn't enough room in the house for both our stuff, so someone's had to go."

"Mine."

"Yours. Oh!" Dolan gestured with his putter. "I hate when the ball gets wedged between the piano's legs. Makes for an inconvenient shot. Can really mess up your handicap."

Barrett seethed. "Father Dolan. We have more important matters to discus—"

"Won't be a minute."

And as Barrett watched, the portly Dolan knelt in a low crouch and tried to duck his head low enough to scuttle under the piano. After a few pained seconds, it became obvious this wouldn't work. Barrett repressed a shudder as Dolan switched tactics, went down on all fours and began crawling.

"Crawling under the piano," said Dolan in a playful sing-song voice. "Here I am aged fifty, crawling under the piano. And you know what? If you had asked me twenty years ago where I saw myself at fifty, I bet I *never* would have said..." (Barrett braced himself against the hated phrase as it returned) "...'crawling under the piano.'"

"As amusing, Father Dolan, as I find your golfing monkeyshines to be—"

"Golf is not monkeyshines, Father Barrett. It's a very serious game."

"Will you get out from under the fucking piano please?"

"Temper." Kneeling, Dolan set up his shot and swung. *Clack.* The golf ball jumped the edge of the carpet and rolled back in range of the high-ball glass. Dolan crawled back out and stood. "Really, Father

Barrett if you don't calm yourself, I'll be forced to ask you to leave."

"Gee. Like piling all my shit at the curb doesn't already send that message…"

"As I said. I was just making *room*. There was no intent to impose any *authority* over the situation." Dolan crouched, sited and putted again. *Clunk!* The ball rolled. "Because of course although I am now, *officially,* the head of this parish, I'm not the type to try and throw my weight around. That strikes me as awfully unnecessary. And, what's more, extremely un-woke."

"Excuse me?"

"In terms of social justice, I mean."

"I'm more interested in justice for me and my stuff that you pitched out onto the curb."

"Well, that's not…"

"How is that not social justice, I ask you?"

"Well, first of all. You have privilege. You're a white male."

"So are you!"

"Ah, but I identify as an oppressed minority."

"Judging by your golf game, let me guess. You're… handicapped? Somehow?"

"Claustrophobic. To be honest."

"You're claustrophobic and you hoard enough stuff to sink the freakin' *Titanic?* Jesus! *What kind of a colossal head-case are you? And how the hell did you end up a priest?"*

"I have an aptitude." *Clunk!*

"That's it," snarled Barrett. He whirled and marched back in the direction of the parish office (which turned out to be blocked by a shelf of canned goods. So he migrated back toward the kitchen, having to double-back past Dolan a second time and then take a short-cut through what he was fairly sure was the dining room). Eventually he spotted a telephone. He grabbed the receiver and punched in the number for the Archdiocese's offices in Vancouver. He followed the phone tree through the menu to Crowe's voicemail box.

"Your Excellency," he said after the tone, "this is Father Michael Barrett calling you from St. Michael's and St. Joan's in Fulton BC. My replacement has arrived. I would appreciate if your Excellency could make some time to mediate on an area of disagreement between us. It has to do with our living arrangements." Barrett was pleasantly surprised by how calm he managed to sound. *Shell-shock, likely,* he thought. He signed off with a request for Crowe's prayerful consideration then hung up. He decided to go back the garage.

What more could Dolan possibly possess? And where had all this stuff come from, anyway? Had Dolan been keeping it all in storage somewhere? It was easily the most colossal collection of useless garbage Barrett had ever come across—a veritable mountain of junk. There was something almost Biblical about it. Barrett narrowed his eyes. He couldn't recall any Biblical stories specifically about hoarders but there was sure plenty about not cleaving to one's possessions. And Dolan's ran the gamut from sets of rusty golf-clubs to bound stacks of newspapers, piles of paperback books, banker's boxes full of files and loose pages, plastic milk crates packed with office supplies, cassette and VHS tapes, sewing kits, plastic bags full of loose change twist-tied shut. And there were shoe boxes as well. Hundreds of them.

Barrett reached the door to the garage and twisted the handle.

Every square inch of the garage was crowded with boat trailers. Barrett gazed out on an array of rowboats, small sailing ships, canoes, two-man electric motor boats. Some, to his disgust, still sported dried seaweed on their bows. He found a narrow path that wound through the collection, followed it to the door and let himself out onto the driveway.

Lunacy!

"Hey, father…"

Barrett turned. It was Scooter, still bandaged, a cast on his broken arm, using his good arm to haul trash to the curb in his housecoat and slippers. He was under doctor's orders, off work for the next month. He tipped a nod at the garage.

"Guess he threw all your stuff out, hey father?"

"Looks that way."

"You can come and stay at my place." Scooter wheeled the plastic bin to the curb and wiped his good hand on his housecoat as he spoke. "Leastways until you get sorted out. Come on. I just bought a whole bunch of frozen hamburger patties and beer."

"Scooter, you're a prince."

The sexton laughed. "Honestly, father, I'd feel better having you around. That Father Dolan, he's crazier than a shit-house rat. Keeps popping out to visit. I'd just as soon not be interrupted. I figure if you're there…" Scooter did not finish his sentence, merely led Barrett around back to the parking lot and made for his fifth-wheel.

"Sergeant Lewis said the same thing." Barrett chuckled. "I guess our Father Dolan isn't afraid to reach out and touch somebody any time of the day or night."

"He's a kook." Scooter padded up the air-stairs to the screen door and tugged it wide. Seating Barrett at the kitchen table, he produced two beers, popped the tabs on both, then shut the door and drew the blinds. There was a light in a recessed nook by the cabinet. When Scooter switched it on, its dull red glow evoked the air of a jazz club, circa 1963. Scooter activated the onboard stereo and slid into the booth across from Barrett. Miles Davis floated from the speakers.

"Must say, Scooter. You know how to live." Barrett admired the effect. "What did you do before this?"

"Same thing, actually." He laughed. "I was the janitor up at the high-school. It was a solid gig. Union. Lasted me until 2012 or so, then I started looking to cash out. This seemed like a graceful step down." Scooter took a good long pull of beer and shook his head. "I've always been a God person. And truth is, I heard and saw a lot working at that high school. Things that are like to change a person."

"How do you mean?"

"I mean youth is a ruthless thing, father." Scooter got serious as Miles drew his sketches of Spain. "I was janitor when most of the current city fathers were in high school. And the generation after, and again after that. I've watched kids grow up and become teachers and politicians and business owners. You know, there's really not that much difference between the in-group in town today and the in-group they were back in high school."

"I believe it."

"Take Jackie, for instance. The girl you rescued the other day." Scooter pointed toward the shuttered window with his beer can. "She went to high-school with the son of the mayor. Kid's now grown up and owns a car dealership. Jackie's still aristocracy, too. If you catch my meaning."

"You mean she was important back in school because of who her dad was?"

"Yeah. Was then. Still is." Scooter dragged a bowl of

chips over. "Never had it easy with her dad, though. He loves her something fierce but he also drives her crazy. Drives her away. She started getting into trouble when she was really young. Like, twelve." Scooter grinned. "Seemed determined to outdo her dad!"

"I can see it. Of course, she could have rebelled by joining the church choir…"

"Not her!" Scooter guffawed. "That goddam girl is hell on wheels! Always has been, always will be! Goes her own way. And she did in high-school. She disappeared a lot. Ran away. Lewis, he was new to town back then, spent many a weekend looking around for Jackie. Of course, I knew where she was. I had friends."

"Where was she?"

Scooter smiled mischievously. "You know that old Anglican cemetery down by the river? She and her friends used to break into the groundsman's cottage. Didn't make any difference. There was nobody there." Scooter shrugged. "Anglicans had given up on the place years before. Paid me to go in and clean up maybe twice a year. That's how I knew about the cottage."

"You say Jackie and her friends hung out there?"

"All the time. It was a sweet deal." Scooter pounded back his beer, rose and hauled two fresh ones from the fridge. "Place still had power and sewage hook-ups. Storm-shutters had been nailed into place on the front windows years back so you could have the entire place lit up at night and no one could see you from the road. She'd stay there with her friends sometimes two, three nights at a stretch in the summer. Drove Lewis bug-fuck."

"You never told him?"

Scooter shook his head. "Look, father. Way I see it is —being a kid sucks. And sometimes all a kid needs is a place to get away and be himself. That's the way I had it figured. Sure, I knew where they were going and what they were up to. And I kept that to myself. Don't get me wrong. If anything bad had ever happened, I would have stepped forward and said something. But nothing ever did."

"How long did kids use that place?"

"It was a twenty-ought thing. Last few years before I was getting set to hang it up and come out here. Say 2008 to 2012. Thereabouts. That would have been when Jackie was, like sixteen, seventeen."

"That was when she was having problems with her dad?"

"The worst problems, yeah. That was when things were at their worst. That's when she spent the most time living in that abandoned cottage down by the river."

Down By The River

SHOES IN HAND, Barrett let himself out onto the air-stairs and closed Scooter's trailer door softly behind him. It was still dark. He figured he couldn't have slept more than three or four hours. In fact, he was still mostly drunk. Which was fine. He was good when he was drunk. Loose. Less apt to become rattled by the unexpected. He sat down on the steps and laced up his shoes.

His friends had done things like camp out by the river back when Barrett was in high-school, so it didn't seem entirely out of character for Jackie to have done likewise. Barrett tried recalling what he could from things his friends had told him of such trips, ignoring the ugly ripple of anger he felt. Managing such ugly ripples was common enough to be reflexive for Barrett, but this time he took stock of the anger. He looked into that dark place inside himself, the one meant to be kept away with violence or wine, drinking until the black mouth of the tunnel appeared, the one that made the world go away, and then diving as far down that tunnel as he possibly could. It was a place he was meant to cross through without looking—definitely without looking down.

It wasn't just that one ripple of anger. It was a carpet of them.

Imagining Jackie and her friends in their junior and senior years of school, Barrett recalled that his own friends had bonded closely with one another by going on these adventures. Slowly, their bonds had deepened to the point at which he suddenly found himself a stranger. And so as high-school ended and his friends moved forward with their lives, they were strengthened by friendships that had started in high-school but which truly blossomed in the years immediately afterwards. Only Barrett had been left outside.

And so Jackie and her friends would have been bonding. The place would have sentimental value. It wouldn't have been easy for Jackie to return, Barrett thought, slipping behind the wheel of the parish Hyundai and starting it up. Knowing the driveway was right below the window of the master bedroom, he revved the engine several times and kicked the headlights up to high-beam as he backed out. Oh-so slowly.

Pre-dawn dark. He saw thick pools of shadow gathering in the low-lying places, under trees and between buildings. The kind of places you could slip into and experience another hour or two of night. Barrett had become very good at finding those during his last two years in high-school, when taking care of his mother often meant staying up into the wee hours, leaving him only a precious three or four to sleep before the demands of breakfast, housekeeping and school would occupy him until his return. Then the round of chores would begin and last late into the evening, interspersed with homework and a hasty dinner.

Poor Jackie, he thought. She would never know the joys of caring for an invalided mother and falling asleep beneath the piano for a faux-night's sleep in the stolen hours before school. Pianos. Shadows. Feasting on scraps from banquets that others take for granted...

Without even glancing at his watch, Barrett knew it would be hours before he could take his first drink of the day.

Fuck.

Fulton was as calm as a dead body in the pre-dawn silence. Barrett had attended many deaths, seen many bodies, conducted many funerals in his time. Such rituals were for the living, not the dead. Friendships and graduations were no different: they benefited only those present to enjoy them. And they served to provide a historical framework explaining the past and everyone's presence in it.

...and the absence of others.

Again, the ripple of anger. He suppressed it.

He could smell the river now. It was somewhere on the other side of the trees. He was imagining teenage Jackie and a handful of friends, perhaps in a pick-up truck, her sitting on a cooler in back in jean shorts and cowboy boots and maybe young Randy lounging somewhere nearby, hoisting a brew, a dim, geekier version of himself, a photographic negative of the foul-mouthed, beer-swilling woman-beater he would become. Doubtless a bunch of similar losers would be nearby, in the cab, behind the wheel, hanging for dear life by the goddam roof-rack, all full of bonhomie and good fellowship.

His mother had died the week of graduation. It didn't matter. He didn't have any plans, anyway. After they took her away, he called and made an appointment at a funeral home for the next afternoon. And then he gathered his bedding—his sheets and duvet his pillows and padded sleeping bag—and laid them out under the piano. Then he drew the curtains and took the phone off the hook and crawled inside and slept for fourteen continuous hours. When he awoke, it was as if his entire childhood had vanished and he was Rip Van Winkle, awaking all alone in a strange land, left behind. And he was trying very hard not to think about any of this as he followed the signs to St. Benedict's Cemetery.

The further he descended into the forest, the more rutted the road became. He could already see traces of the teenage party Mecca the cemetery had become. The Anglicans had totally let the place go to hell, but he supposed that fit. The Anglican Church had been founded on the basis of sin—that of divorce. Specifically, the divorce of one fat English king with a fondness for other men's wives. No sooner was old King Henry finished with one wife than he wanted another. So it was with the church he founded: always starting things and never following through. Just like this damned cemetery.

He found a dirt parking circle at the bottom of the forested foothills and parked beneath a low-hanging tangle of Spanish Moss dangling from a massive oak. With the engine off and the window rolled down, Barrett could see nothing—only puddled shadows of night lingering in amongst the trees and distant suggestions of a structure. And here he was, concealed beneath the Spanish moss, drinking in the remains of pre-dawn dark, like he had under the pian—

Stop it. For Christ's sake, stop thinking about it.

He slid from the car, flashed on his mental image of teen Jackie and her friends, then of his own friends right before they abandoned him, and managed not to slam the driver's door shut.

The stone path to the rusted cemetery gate was almost completely overgrown. Barrett had to bushwhack his way through tall grass, fallen branches, blackberry bushes that grasped at his trousers. He picked his way through the cluster of tombstones. The gate itself was almost completely overgrown and the tombstones, some of which dated to the 1940s, were choked among dense-packed grass and brambles. But the grass was compressed ahead, twisting in a worn ribbon between the graves. Barrett noted the fast-food drink cups, empty beer cans and cigarette packs littering the edges of the path. Teen central. *I didn't miss much,* he told himself.

A building appeared up ahead through the trees. One of those tin gardening sheds you can buy at the hardware store. And beyond that, a simple cottage. Barrett could see the storm shutters nailed into place on the front windows and the electrical box in back, cables running from it directly to a small phone pole nearby. Somewhere through the trees' distance, it linked up with the main power lines. But this was the only junction box for miles. At first blush, the thing seemed to be in working order. But the nearest window—one which appeared to lead into a small utility closet—was busted out, its glass scattered on the lawn at the building's edge.

Barrett walked around to the side of the building. Three steps led up to a side door, open to the kitchen. Cupboards stood open and empty and a thick black smear on the wall behind the stove testified to cooking experiments that had gone entirely wrong. The sink was full of empty tin cans: beans, ravioli, soup. Barrett was taking the short entry hall from the kitchen to the front room when the sound of Harleys broke the silence.

He went quickly back through the kitchen to the door, down the steps and into the trees behind the house, taking refuge behind a thick bush as the Harleys cut out and voices rose. Barrett strained to hear what they were saying but, at this distance, he couldn't even be sure they were speaking English. Very soon after—alarmingly so—a figure appeared at the open kitchen door and scanned the yard and environs. His survey passed right by Barrett's position without noticing. Here was a biker, alright. But not one of Mick's boys. These two were Huns.

Interesting…

Voices again, this time in the kitchen. Barrett caught the words '*shit*' and '*clean up.*' They gave no indication of suspecting his presence. He had not been trying deliberately to conceal the car but was now glad he had parked under the tree. The Spanish Moss must have done a better job concealing the Hyundai than he imagined possible.

What the hell are they doing in there? Barrett couldn't understand why the Huns would bother to clean up. Had they spent the night there? If so, how many of them? Had Jackie been with them?

No sooner had Barrett formulated the question when he experienced one of his intuitions. He hadn't felt that fluttering in the stomach, that warming at the base of the deck since his days as a cop in Toronto but he recognized it immediately. His danger signal. His clue that he had left something—

My phone!

– neglected something potentially—

What if it rings?

…dangerous.

He reached at the exact moment he felt the trembling, the warming in his pocket that presaged a call. His thumb reached the volume button at the same instant one of the bikers appeared on the steps holding a plastic bag of garbage. Barrett crammed the volume button against the phone as hard and fast as he could. Holding his breath and counting he detected a weak buzz right before it went completely silent. One second later and the phone would have rung, revealing his position. As the biker gathered bits of garbage from the yard, Barrett pulled his phone from his pocket and noted the message light blinking. Someone had left a voicemail.

Barrett turned and pressed his back against the thick trunk of a cedar and slid down until his butt touched his heels. He remained there, breathing hard until the Harleys started up again and roared off back into the forest. Barrett stayed put for another twenty minutes before venturing forth.

The Huns had cleaned the sexton's cottage out, soup to nuts. The kitchen was spotless. Every stray can and scrap of paper had been lifted and removed, windows closed and curtains drawn. Like they were getting ready for a home inspection. Removing every trace...

They don't want anyone to know they've been here.

Barrett hurried out front. Sure enough, there were deep impressions in the gravel where their Harleys had rested, but Barrett could tell they had taken care to guide their bikes out along the grassy verge where they left no trace. Following their progress, he could see the Hyundai was completely concealed by Spanish Moss from this angle. Satisfied they were gone, Barrett drew out his phone and checked voicemail. It was a man's voice, a number and a request for a call back. He hit the redial button. The caller answered after two rings.

"McLean's Funeral Home."

"This is Michael Barrett from St. Michael's and St. Joan's parish, returning your call."

"Oh, father. Thanks. I'm David McLean, funeral director. Father, could you come to the funeral home at once? We have an emergency."

"Sure." Barrett frowned and pulled out his car keys. "What's up?"

"Someone dumped a body here overnight, father. Seemed appropriate to contact a priest. How soon can you get here?"

Delivery

"FOUND IT BACK HERE, FATHER." The maintenance woman in the jumpsuit led Barrett across the narrow porch from the rear door of McLean's Funeral Home to the dumpsters. The name patch on her jumpsuit said 'Lori' and the funeral director had spoken to her in a way that suggested they were family. *Daughter probably,* thought Barrett. He had no way of knowing for sure. In his five weeks in Fulton, Barrett had yet to deal with the local funeral home but it seemed like a reasonable conjecture.

"What time you find it?" Barrett asked.

"When I started, just about an hour back. Seven-thirty AM." She gave a low chuckle. "I've heard of them dumping guys at the Emergency Room, but never a funeral home."

"Probably too late for ER." Barrett knelt to examine the ground by the dumpsters. "Where was he?"

"On top of the dumpster. Here. Well, half-on. The other part of him was hanging here." She scuffed the ground with a boot. Barrett looked. Nothing remarkable.

Cement. Some dirt. Some crumpled leaves. *But no trees around here.* That was significant. He rose, brushing his hands together. "Take me to him."

Lori sighed and shuffled back to the door. Following her inside, Barrett side-stepped the janitorial cart where it sat obstructing the hallway entrance and then tracked her down a dark corridor to a room hovering in the smell of steel and chemicals. Inside stood a gloved man in a face mask and hospital scrubs. Behind him, wearing a dark suit and steel-rimmed glasses was the funeral director.

"Father Barrett, this gentleman is with the BC Coroner's Service. Before he conducts his exam, I was wondering if you would mind taking a look at the cadaver. Perhaps you'd recognize him."

"I'll take a look." Barrett's eyes and nose were watering. *Christ, he's ripe!* McLean thoughtfully offered a fresh set of nose-plugs in a plastic blister pack. Barrett put them on and stepped over to the table. The coroner peeled back the body bag. Barrett stared down at Randy's whitened, shrivelled face.

"Christ," he muttered, turning away. He stepped to the door, pulled it open and slumped against the hallway wall.

"Father?" McLean stepped out, pulling the door shut behind him. "You know him?"

"He's officially a missing person." Barrett's head was reeling. "His name's Randy. Sergeant Lewis from the RCMP is looking for him."

"Well..." McLean seemed to be at a loss. "Well, then I suppose we should call the detachment right away..."

"Not so fast." Barrett pushed away panicked thoughts of his St. Ignatius medal and drew a deep breath. "Do you have any CCTV coverage on this building?"

"Sure. All over the place." McLean seemed a little suspicious of Barrett's hesitancy to involve the law. "You want to check the rear cameras?"

"I'm thinking. Yeah." Barrett glanced around. "Where's the, ah—"

"Control console? It's in the systems room."

Like any modern business, McLean's funeral home had a small enclosed space set aside for racks of servers and modems. This one might have started life as a broom closet. A flatscreen PC monitor and keyboard occupied a desk in the back corner. McLean stepped over and hauled out the chair.

"Insurance company demanded we set all this up," he grumbled, seizing the mouse and jabbing the keyboard with a stubby finger. "Because of health codes pushing up our premiums. Requiring us to install a generator in case the power went down and we had cadavers on ice. It happens." He swirled the mouse on its Cooper Funeral Caskets, Inc. mousepad. A program window appeared in a split-screen, 9-camera array. Along the right side was a panel containing a series of toggles and switches for manipulating the digital archive stream.

"How long does the footage stay in storage?" Barrett craned over McLean's shoulder and squinted at the images. He saw the alley and the silhouette of the wall's edge at the rear of the property.

"Forty-five days." McLean was toggling the timer to replay everything from midnight onward. "About twelve-thirty is when the security car comes by. Let's see…" He tapped the mouse to speed up the film. Darkness flickered as wind subtly readjusted trees, bushes, signs and laundry-lines, causing the light to shift at high speed. A bright blob appeared at the head of the alley and approached a cluster of shadows that turned out to be the dumpsters. The rear camera afforded them a wide-angle view of the whole scene.

"That's Jamie," said McLean. "He's a guard with Fulton Security, Ltd. See, he's getting out and tugging on the gate to make sure it's locked? The gate is there to make sure the dumpsters don't get stolen. Okay, so Jamie rattles the gate… Gets back in his car… Makes a note on his clipboard and… Drives away."

The headlights floated off, stage right, returning the dumpsters to shadow. McLean sped up the tape. Barrett saw, again: wind-shifted light and undulating shadows. A second blob of lights appeared, slowing near the gate. Barrett could discern a tall silver hood ornament.

"That a Jag?" he asked.

"Hm. Looks to be. Oh, and lookee here. This gentleman decided to…urinate outside the funeral home."

"You can speed past this part."

McLean went through at double speed, watching the obviously relieved man tuck himself in before returning behind the wheel of his Jag and floating away as the security car had done, re-draping the dumpsters in their cowl of shadows. They dominated the screen. McLean and Barrett waited.

Then: a thin sliver of light. It beamed bright before fading again. A single headlight, followed by another.

"Motorcycles," muttered Barrett.

McLean glanced at him. "Makes sense," he mumbled. "Now look. There's…looks like another car."

The two Huns parked their bikes on the far side of the alley in full view of the camera, then moved toward the shadowed hulk of the vehicle hidden in the powerful glare of its own headlights. The men's shadows merged behind the glare. They returned, carrying a load draped over their shoulders. They tried to pitch it over the wall but it flew lopsided and landed halfway on—and halfway off—the dumpster. McLean hit the pause button on the control panel.

"We've got to call Lewis." Barrett managed to keep his voice level. "Can I use your office?"

"Certainly, father. Help yourself."

He went down the hall into the main executive office and closed the double doors behind him. Alone, he slumped against the wall, his hands over his face. The tension in his chest unclenched and he loosed a long, slow exhale, knees trembling. A kind of crazed euphoria swept over him making him briefly light-headed and he had to catch himself against the wall with one hand.

He was in the clear.

Randy had been found.

It was over.

There was no telling who was behind the stunt with his St. Ignatius medal but that didn't matter now. What mattered was getting himself off of Lewis' list of suspects. He moved toward McLean's vast rosewood desk with its ornate phone. One of those retro jobs, with a big solid handle and a rope cord, like something a World War I general might use to order a cavalry charge. Barrett reached for the thing before remembering that he had Lewis' number programmed into his cell and used that instead.

An answer after two rings: "Fulton RCMP."

"Lewis, it's Barrett. I found Randy."

"Jesus Christ! Where are you?"

"McLean's Funeral Home."

Silence. Then:

"Did you kill him, padre?"

"No. But whoever did dumped him over the back fence at three o'clock this morning. We have video."

"I'll be right down."

Barrett took another minute to calm himself before opening the twin doors of the large executive office. McLean was standing right outside, eyes narrowed, a question on his face. He had been suspicious when Barrett asked him to hold off on calling RCMP. And now that suspicion was back. Barrett could sense it lurking.

"Is he coming, father? You spoke to Sergeant Lewis, correct?"

"The very man." Barrett punched his open palm with a fist. "Say, Mr. McLean. You wouldn't happen to have anything to drink around here would you?"

"Well, I don't… No, not really. Besides, it's only nine o'clock in the morning and the police are on their way."

Christ, if he wasn't suspicious before, he certainly is now. Barrett wondered if he'd have to kill McLean. He wasn't above doing it if necessary but he really didn't want to.

This was shaping up to be one hell of a morning.

Lewis arrived twenty minutes later. McLean conducted them back to the systems closet and re-ran the CCTV footage. Lewis had him pause on the first frame containing a biker and jabbed a finger at the screen.

"How can you be sure those are Huns, padre?"

"It's the shape of the patch. Rounded. The Paladins wear a diamond-shaped patch. You can see—there—in the light from the streetlamp." Barrett pointed. "There."

"Okay, let's say those are Huns badges. Or patches. Whatever they're called. We can't positively ID those guys based on this footage alone. You know that."

"That's not the point. The point is, the Huns were somehow involved in Randy's disappearance. Also, somehow, in his death." *Nice out there Barrett,* the priest congratulated himself. Every word he had just said was absolutely true. The Huns certainly *had* helped Randy vanish (albeit, after his death, and so it was something of a stretch to say they had something to do with his death, but it was semantically correct). Now Lewis could head off and investigate the Huns and leave Barrett and the Paladins in peace.

But Lewis was having none of it. He was examining Barrett suspiciously. So was McLean.

Great! Barrett thought. Suddenly he was a suspect. Or, at the very least, suspicious.

"Look." He took Lewis by the elbow and steered him into McLean's office, shutting the door behind them. "This fits with what I learned earlier today."

"Which is?"

"There's an old cemetery down by the river. St. Benedict's. The Anglican one. You know it? Anyway, Jackie used to hang out there when she was in high-school. So I went down to investigate."

"Good." Lewis' tone held real approval. "And what did you find?"

"There was evidence of squatters in the sexton's cottage. I saw a couple of Huns show up and begin cleaning up the place. Carted out all the trash, covering their tracks as they went."

"So, they've been using it."

"And there's no *question* that's them dumping off Randy's body! Gavin, I'm certain of it. I think I even recognize that one guy. But even if I can't, it's a pretty solid investigative lead, wouldn't you agree?"

"Unless you're hiding something."

"*What?*" Barrett was jolted as if by electric shock. "*Hiding* something? Like *what?*"

"What was in that envelope Walton gave you at the station?"

"A private letter from a parishioner who didn't want her husband to know she had contacted me." The lie came to Barrett's lips effortlessly, seemingly from out of nowhere, and dropped into the conversation with absolute conviction. At least he had that going for him.

Thank you, Jesus...

Lewis continued staring at Barrett wordlessly for a few seconds. "Okay," he said. "Yes. It is a lead. I'll get into it. But you've still got work to do. I need to know where Jackie is."

"I'm on it. You know I can get results. I've proven that."

"You have indeed."

"So?" Barrett crossed his arms. "Where's my money?"

Lewis examined Barrett as if the priest were some weird form of marine life he had just found in his coffee. Then, heaving a deep sigh, he produced his wallet and drew a check out from among the folded bills.

"There you go, padre. First week's wages."

Barrett pocketed the check without glancing at it. He let himself out past Lori, who was vacuuming the reception area. The sun blazed overhead, dazzling his eyes. Barrett blinked, fished out sunglasses and shoved them into place. Then he walked back to the parish house, breathing slowly and figuring out his next move. He decided to wait until eleven before having his first drink. That seemed eminently fair and reasonable under the circumstances and Barrett congratulated himself on his restraint.

The parish house driveway had been cleared of everything. A black car was parked beside Father Dolan's station wagon. Barrett noted a chauffeur sitting behind the wheel, reading a newspaper. As Barrett made his way to the house, the front door opened.

"Ah. Father Barrett." Archbishop Crowe blinked owlishly behind the thick frames of his eyeglasses. "We've been waiting for you."

Inquisition

"I WAS VERY concerned when I received Father Dolan's voicemail. Well…voice*mails,* actually…"

"Oh?" Barrett noted the front sitting room was suspiciously neat and clear of debris. Dolan who sat piously on the edge of the couch, back straight, as alert and on edge as if he were a visitor in his own home. "How many did he send?"

"Not many," Dolan piped up. "Only about five."

"I see. Looks like you've cleaned up, Father Dolan." Barrett cast around for a place to sit and decided on the recliner. "Didn't you have your record collection piled on this chair when I left this morning?"

"Oh, goodness no." Dolan uttered a jag of panicked laughter that reminded Barrett of a poodle's bark. "That's in the garage."

Along with all my stuff, Barrett thought. Seething, he managed to settle himself, smile pleasantly and restrain a strong desire to rip out Dolan's teeth with extreme prejudice. Archbishop Crowe, meanwhile, perched on the love-seat, leaned back and crossed his arms.

"So the reason I've come, at your mutual request, is apparently there seems to be some *conflict* between the two of you—"

"Father Barrett has been *extremely* hostile. I'm sorry to interrupt, your Excellency, but I've been simply *bursting* with discontent. And an inability to express my dissatisfaction because, well, honestly? May I be honest? Father Barrett has been less than *charitable* in his conduct. He's been inhospitable, critical, condemnatory, and downright *ungracious* in his behavior toward me." Dolan flashed what was supposed to be a sad smile. "I think he's taking his removal as head of this parish quite, well...*personally*."

Barrett gritted his teeth. Why did these stupid political battles always proceed the same way? The liar and the opportunist teaming up to wreak havoc on people like Barrett who just want to be left alone. Because more than anything right now he just wanted to just be left alone. And to have a drink. He checked his watch. It was quarter to ten. He began inwardly walking back his eleven o'clock resolution.

Meanwhile, Dolan wanted a reaction. So Barrett sat there silently.

"Father Barrett, do you have anything to say in response?"

"I accept your Excellency's decision to replace me as head of this parish."

"I see." Crowe's eyes slid toward Dolan, who chose that moment to ponder the contents of his coffee cup. "So, what is the source of your personal difficulty with Father Dolan?"

"I have none, your Grace. I requested your assistance in resolving some issues related to housing. That Father

Dolan sees this as a personal conflict is a complete surprise to me."

"I see." Crowe turned to Dolan. "Father Dolan, let me ask you. What efforts have you made to clear the air with Father Barrett?"

"I *told* you, your Grace! Father Barrett has been unrelentingly *hostile* and *critical* of my presence here. He—"

"Father Dolan."

"—he has just been so unwelcoming and—"

"Father Dolan."

"—I've *never* encountered *anything* like—"

"Father *Dolan.*" Crowe sat forward and smiled after raising his voice slightly. "Let's back up here a little bit. How do *you* feel about your assignment here?"

Dolan jerked to an abrupt halt. "Uh? Feel? Well, aside from Father Barrett's *continuous* hostility and lack of—"

"Let's *leave* Father Barrett out of this for a moment, shall we?" For the first time since meeting the Archbishop, Barrett sensed a hint of frustration bubbling up from behind Crowe's calm façade. "Let's just talk about your own relationship to this parish and your vocation."

"Your Excellency?"

"Perhaps it is *you* who are being condemnatory and ungracious. Perhaps you took your own removal from this parish as personally as you try to claim Father Barrett is."

"Of course, I understand your Excellency's perspective. It is a reasonable conclusion, all things considered. But, Archbishop…please understand." Dolan paused, dropped his gaze to the rug and swallowed. "It wasn't *me*. It was the parishioners here. Until Father Barrett came, I was beginning to cultivate a following among the local native population. But my removal derailed the initiative. And Father Barrett has sown nothing but discord between the church and the local First Nations."

"What?" Barrett actually laughed out loud. "What the hell are you talking about?"

"Your Excellency, when I arrived there was a death threat spray-painted on the side of the church. Our sexton, who was assaulted when he caught the vandal in the act and was taken by ambulance to the hospital, confirmed it was done by the local Indian youth. You see? It's proof Father Barrett has been irresponsible in his handling of First Nation outreach."

Crowe considered for almost a full minute.

"A church worker was attacked and hospitalized and this is the first I'm hearing of it? Father Barrett?"

"Ah, you removed and replaced me, your Excellency. Remember?"

"Of course I remember. But—Oh, never mind. Father Dolan?"

"Yes, your Excellency?"

"Why is this—"

"Your Excellency, *mea culpa* and forgive me. It's my most grievous fault. But I was overwhelmed, you see, by Father Barrett's unrelenting criticisms and—"

"How is Scooter?" Crowe turned to Barrett.

"He's fine, thank you, Archbishop. I spent last night in his trailer, in fact. Can I, ah offer your Excellency some refreshment? Some coffee perhaps? Or—" (a glance at his watch) "—wine, maybe? I think I may have a glass of wine…"

"Father Barrett, sit down. Look, I want you to make all the arrangements for Scooter. We'll have someone from Human Resources stop by and square away his disability situation. And I want him to have paid time off. That man's been with us a good long time and I want to make sure he's taken care of." Crowe threw a disappointed glance Dolan's way. "Now Father Barrett, please fill me in on the status of your relations with the local First Nations, if you'd be so kind. As you know, the Diocese is legally and morally committed to Reconciliation…"

"It seems, Archbishop that—"

"Father Barrett has an awful relationship with the local tribe, your Excellency. He's been in street brawls with the local youth…"

"Father Dolan?"

"Yes?"

"Would you go fetch us a pot of coffee, please? And anything you might have to eat. It's been a long drive from the airport."

After an awkward hesitation, Dolan rose. "Of course, your Excellency. I'll put together some sandwiches."

"Sounds wonderful."

Dolan stood perfectly still for a long handful of seconds. Then he turned and moved jerkily from the room.

"Father Barrett…" The Archbishop sat forward, his expression thoughtful. "First of all, I'm disinclined to accept that you're entirely to blame for the present situation. But from the standpoint of public relations, we have to pull back and reconsider our position. If there's a problem between you and any local First Nations, I want it handled, understood?"

"Yes, your Excellency."

Dolan suddenly returned. He must have had a pot of coffee going in the kitchen because he carried a tray containing cookies, cream, sugar, and, Barrett noted, three cups of coffee. He began speaking as he set down the tray.

"I couldn't help overhearing your Excellency's instruction to Father Barrett to 'handle' the situation with our Native friends. Allow me to say, Archbishop, that that might be a big mistake. A *very* big mistake, indeed."

"Father Dolan—"

"*Please,* your Excellency. Allow me to explain. The graffiti on the church was left because of the ill will Father Barrett has sown. I think he would only exacerbate tensions by being left in charge of the relationship with the local band."

"Father Dolan, please…"

"Archbishop, please. Allow *me* to mediate Father Barrett's rapprochement with the tribe. I think—"

"Father Dolan, thank you very much. We have instructions for you."

"Archbishop?"

"Go and take some coffee and a plate of cookies out to my chauffer, please. Then consult your parish archives and ensure that all birth certificates are refiled in alphabetical order as opposed to date of birth."

"Ah, *now?*"

"I would prefer if you started at once, yes."

Dolan stood so motionless that Barrett couldn't tell if he was even breathing. It was as if Dolan were giving the universe the benefit of the doubt, the chance to stop in its tracks and reverse Crowe's decision, change the direction fate had decided to go. But the moment came and went and he was still standing there and nothing had changed. So he exhaled, turned and stalked from the room, muttering, "Yes, your Excellency."

The door swung shut behind Dolan and Crowe

breathed a sigh of what seemed to Barrett to be one of absolute relief.

"How has your experience of Father Dolan been, Father Barrett?"

"Ah…fine? Your Excellency? I suppose. He *is* a trifle…let's say 'eccentric.'"

"Quite. But the two of you are cohabiting smoothly?"

"Um, well. No, your Excellency. That was why I requested your assistance. It seems that Father Dolan has laid up much treasure in worldly goods."

"How do you mean?" Crowe sipped his coffee crossly. "Speak plainly, Father Barrett."

"He's got a lot of stuff, Archbishop. So much that he's effectively crowded me out of the house."

"Crowded you…?" Crowe set down his coffee cup with a *click*. "Where are you…? Is that why you spent the night in Scooter's trailer?"

"Yes, your Excellency."

Crowe loosed a frustrated sigh. "I see. And where are your belongings at present?"

"Stored in the garage, I believe, your Excellency."

"Good Lord." Crowe's voice sounded small—defeated, almost. "Alright. You'll move out of Scooter's trailer at once. The archdiocese will pay for hotel accommodations. Just set yourself up somewhere reasonable and forward us an expense report. We'll reimburse you."

"Thank you, your Excellency."

Crowe rose and moved to the bay window, staring out at the street.

"It's really a shame," he said at last. "I'm very fond of this church. You see, I did a stint here back in the 1970s, not long after I was ordained. It's always mattered to me that there's competent leadership at this parish. The simple truth is that I'll never close it. No matter how much pressure I receive, no matter how precipitously the congregation may dwindle. St. Michael's and St. Joan's Church will always be a part of daily life here in Fulton. For that reason, I won't allow it to ever be too terribly mishandled before stepping in. It's always helpful to know who's hopeless at running a parish and…who isn't."

Crowe turned.

"Father, I want you to seek out the Chief of the local band and affect a Reconciliation with him. It's extremely important that we remain on good terms with the local First Nations, so I am directing you to take this step. Explain to the Chief that this is at your Archbishop's direction. Please tell him to feel free to call me."

"Yes, your Excellency."

"And thank you, Father Barrett, for keeping an eye on Scooter for us."

"Of course."

————

BARRETT STEPPED INTO THE GARAGE. Sidling his way between Father Dolan's collection of boats on boat trailers, he dug through a chest of drawers until locating a plain green duffle bag. Switching drawers, he began grabbing handfuls of clean socks and underwear and cramming them into the bag. His cell chimed as he was hunting for trousers.

"Father Barrett here."

"It's Lewis. We need to sit down and compare notes on a few things."

"Sure thing. When?"

"Let's meet for drinks later tonight. Say around seven at the Junction?"

"I'll be there."

Barrett checked his watch. Not quite eleven. But he went and poured that glass of wine just the same.

No-Tell Motel

BARRETT SHUT the closet door and tossed the empty duffle bag onto the bathroom counter, then unwrapped a drinking glass from its antiseptic paper envelope and sat on the lumpy mattress to pour himself some wine from the box on the bedside table. He swung his legs up onto the duvet and toasted his new digs Unit 426 of the Fulton Arms Motor Hotel, and drank. The wine went down surprisingly smooth for a Chateau Vintage Cardboard Box. Barrett counted his blessings that he had managed to pick out a particularly good batch.

Peace at last.

He was almost ten grand to the good, plus his paycheck from the church. He would likely be on administrative leave for the foreseeable future, although something told him that Archbishop Crowe wouldn't be moving him out of Fulton anytime soon. He had a feeling the Archbishop wanted to keep him around in case…

In case what? Dolan turned out to be every bit the

fuck-up Barrett already knew him to be? Crowe couldn't possibly keep Barrett here. Not after what he'd done to Randy. Besides, Barrett was itching to get back to the Curia, back into full investigative swing, tracking down pedos and…

You realize they may never let you do that again, right?

Why was his damn drinking glass empty? Of all the moments for it to run dry, it chose this one. Unbelievable! Barrett poured himself a tall one, drank deeply and settled the glass on his chest, closing his eyes.

So what if?

He couldn't imagine spending the rest of his life in this shit-hole. But that might be exactly what Crowe had in mind for him. Crowe's little speech about how St. Michael's and St. Joan's would always remain open no matter how much attendance shrank was every bit as horrifying as it was meant to be reassuring. Fulton could easily become Barrett's Elba, his Alcatraz, his St. Helena, his Chateau d'If.

I'll spend the rest of my days helping out Lewis and Walton with their backwoods investigations. Barrett finished a glass and checked his watch. He supposed, shrugging into his jacket and kicking on his shoes, he could spend his life in worse ways. The problem was he just didn't care about the town. Not the way Dolan obviously did. Or pretended to.

Barrett checked his hair in the mirror, then let himself out. The parking lot was deserted save for a gold pick-up parked in front of another unit a few doors down. The Junction was across the street and up a block so he left the Hyundai where it was and opted for a walk. A sharp breeze whisked the parking lot. Barrett buttoned his jacket and jammed his hands in his pockets, tucking his chin against the cold and following his breath out across the silent main drag and up the sidewalk toward the bar.

Funny thing, he thought. *Haven't seen those Indian kids on their bikes for a while. Wonder what the hell happened to them?* Perhaps they'd all been shipped off to some Native boot-camp somewhere for self-improvement purposes. Lord knows they weren't the only ones in Fulton who could use it, Barrett thought, stepping around a little cluster of homeless youth crowding the sidewalk: dreadlocks, blank stares and a girl positioning a syringe near a vein in her forearm. Barrett instinctively looked away.

This town is hell.

But then, perhaps every town is.

Lewis was alone in the bar when Barrett arrived. The wind picked up the moment he walked in, rattling the windows and sweeping the eaves like a bone whistle. With a wave he crossed the empty dance floor and took a seat by Lewis at the bar.

"Thank God we had this appointment," Barrett said. "Because I really need to switch from wine to beer for a while."

"Variety is healthy," Lewis agreed. "Got a head start on me, huh?"

"Unless you've been drinking. Which I'm guessing you haven't. Being in the middle of an investigation and all."

"So are you."

"I've proven I can drink and get results." The blonde bearded barkeep walked in through the batwing doors from the kitchen. "Pint of that pale ale you stock, please."

"Sure thing. Gavin?"

"The usual."

He set them up—a pint for Barrett, a bottle of Grenville Island for Lewis. Then he left them alone.

"Walton and I have been doing a lot of digging into Jackie's past. Tried to run down her mother. No easy task. Jackie herself has always kept a tight circle of friends. That high-school period where she was hanging out in the groundskeeper's house by the cemetery was probably her most active. Since then, aside from her sister and a few of the bikers' girlfriends, she doesn't talk to anybody. And she chooses her friends well."

Barrett nodded, knowing this meant that no one was talking.

"Meanwhile there's this drama between the Paladins and the Huns to worry about. Walton and I have our hands full. I hope you've got something, padre, because we're all fresh out of leads."

"Not really, no. But well, maybe…"

"What's up?"

Barrett chugged his pint and signalled for another. "I have kind of a favor to ask. My boss was here. Archbishop Crowe. He's ordered me to seek out the head of the local tribe and make a gesture of reconciliation."

Lewis considered this in silence for a time. Then he took a sip of his Granville Island and muttered, "Good Christ."

"What?"

"I can see the church is covering its bases. And that's good." Lewis sipped and pulled a face. "But you're going in there to discuss being attacked by kids from his tribe. That's effectively accusing his youngsters of doing something that you can't prove they did. I know, I know… Why shouldn't he believe you? But think about the politics of the thing for a moment. From his point-of-view, you'd be going after his tribe. You're inviting a lawsuit."

"I've heard that somewhere before. Okay, what if we spun it a different way. What if we just said the Bishop is sending me as a gesture of goodwill and concern. Not even mention the incident. Let the Chief bring it up. Or not."

"Or just skip the whole thing altogether…"

"I can't." Barrett smirked. "Archbishop Crowe has ordered me to do this. And Dolan will be checking up on me and tell him right away if I haven't."

"Right. Dolan's back." Lewis got out his cell phone and switched it off. "Thanks for reminding me."

"Sure. Listen, Gavin… I need to do this… Can you…?"

Lewis chuckled. "Set it up you can basically go in there and apologize for getting beaten up? Sure."

"Um, thanks." Barrett wasn't quite sure how to feel about Lewis' characterization of the thing but was grateful the meeting would be arranged.

"Okay." Lewis emptied his beer, thumped the bar twice and stood. "You keep looking for Jackie. We'll talk again." He peeled a ten from his billfold. "This round's on me."

"Thanks."

Barrett watched Lewis cross the dance floor and exit. The door closed and he was alone.

He returned to his earlier musings. So what if the Curia didn't bring him back? And so what if they left him under Archbishop Crowe's authority and Crowe kept him here? Barrett pondered the possibility of living a life of a semi-retired, part-time investigator with occasional clerical duties. Such a life, he reflected, would not be totally unbearable. Plenty of time to drink and reflect.

He suspected he could transform his room at the Fulton Arms into a passable apartment.

I'll have to see if I can pick up a hot-plate at the thrift store, he thought, finishing his beer and rising to go. He was ready to switch back to wine.

The temperature had dropped and the wind was blowing more fiercely on the way back. Barrett glanced up and down the silent streets. No activity at the RCMP detachment or in front of any of the darkened boutiques lining the main drag. Even the alleys were devoid of life. And Barrett caught no sign of the junkies he had passed earlier.

Either they've taken cover in a doorway or dumpster somewhere or have found their way to the shelter. He knew the city ran a shelter the next block over. His church *(no, Dolan's church)* made sack lunches for them once a week. Barrett had never actually visited but had intended to get around to it. It occurred to him it might be a good place to look for Jackie and made a mental note to follow up on it in the morning.

He crossed the motel parking lot, empty save for the gold truck by the unit a few doors down from his. Barrett let himself in, doffed his coat, turned up the heat and poured himself a glass of wine. Then he switched off the lights and stood drinking by the window. He was so settled in the stillness bathing the parking lot outside that he was alerted by the sound of a door opening and closing. That would be the unit with the gold pick-up truck, Barrett thought, sipping wine. He heard footsteps scuffing the gravel and, a moment later, Jackie stepped into view.

Jesus! Barrett put his glass down on the windowsill so hard he spilled some wine. He reached for his phone to call Lewis before remembering that he'd doffed his jacket. Unfortunate, but he sure as hell wasn't about to take his eyes off Jackie. Not now.

She paused by the gold pick-up truck and opened the side door. Barrett watched her produce her purse and sling it over one shoulder before slamming the door. Then she hiked a few steps into the lot, produced a pack of cigarettes and lighter, and lit up. She dragged and blew. Checked her watch.

Waiting for someone, Barrett realized. He seized the opportunity to glide back to his jacket, fish out his phone and return to the window. Jackie was exactly where he'd left her. He dialed Lewis' number and got voicemail.

"Barrett here. Call me right away. I caught sight of Jackie from my motel window. I'm staying at the Fulton Arms, Unit 426. I've got eyes on. I'll keep you informed."

Jackie stiffened and craned forward, peering into the dark. A figure materialized in the street riding a bicycle. Barrett started when he realized…

It's one of those damn Indian kids.

The kid on the bike pedalled across the lot, stopping a short distance from Jackie. His hands fell from the handlebars to settle on his thighs. He said something and Jackie dug out her cigarettes and gave him one. Lit it for him. They talked. Barrett frowned.

The pieces just didn't hang together.

Here was this kid who had helped spray-paint a death threat on his church talking to the missing person he had been sent to investigate. That coincidence was enough to spook him. Nevertheless, he was more determined than ever to get to the bottom of things.

Finding out who owns that gold pick-up truck would be

a good start. He made a mental note to jot down the license plate.

Meanwhile, Jackie and the native kid were finishing their cigarettes and crushing them out. Barrett sensed they were going before either of them made a move. He watched them cross the parking lot. Once they had achieved a safe distance he let himself out and followed.

Weakest Link

AND AWAY WE GO...

Into the night.

For the first minute or so, Barrett considered turning back for the Hyundai. But using the car would make him stick out like a sore thumb. Jackie was walking, the kid pedaling just ahead of her, and they moved at only a slightly faster-than-normal pedestrian pace. Barrett hung a block behind and stuck close to the wall. During his time on the force, he had been a general duty patrolman. Surveillance had not generally been part of his duty due to his uniform.

Still in uniform now. And I probably stick out even worse than a cop. He turned up his lapel to conceal the white square of his clerical collar.

The pair crossed a set of railroad tracks and angled toward the industrial zone. Only a few square blocks in area, the zone was where the construction and trucking firms occupied strip mall space alongside machine shops. It was a grim neighborhood of repair bays and chemical storage facilities. Pollutants crowded the air. Barrett had driven through earlier that morning, so was only slightly surprised when Jackie and friend angled toward McLean's Funeral Home.

Okay.

Now it was starting to come together.

The pair moved quickly, speeding up with each step until they were hurrying. They definitely knew the area, had been here together before. Barrett thought back to the pick-up truck from the CCTV security video and mused about the gold truck in the motel lot. It, along with Jackie and the kid on the bike, were somehow tied in with the theft of Randy's body.

Jackie and the kid stopped in the street before the darkened funeral home. They weren't there long before a handful of other rez kids on bikes appeared. They gathered below the sign that said MCLEAN'S and conversed excitedly. Something had evidently happened here in which they had all taken part. Barrett was starting to sense the contours of the thing.

Why *wouldn't* Jackie care about the disposition of Randy's mortal remains? It made sense that she would. She'd obviously given a shit about his body in life, so why not in death? She had either participated in or more likely seen the dumping of Randy's body here. But was it done by her? And if not, then…

By whom?

The confab continued another five minutes. Barrett didn't register the rumbling rising behind him until it was almost too late. Fortunately, there was a short flight of stairs down from the sidewalk to the fire door of a welding shop. Barrett saw the shadow of the biker appear in the distance behind him and managed to scuttle down the steps before the Harley's headlights reached him. The bike thundered by, deafeningly loud. Barrett stuck his head up from the stairwell. It was a Hun and not a Paladin. He glided around the group of kids in a wide semi-circle before pulling in, wheel-first, and gearing down the Harley to a low rumble.

Okay, *this* was interesting.

Barrett ducked back down. There was nothing to hear, and he had already seen everything there was to see: Jackie, allied with those Indian kids, was meeting up with a member of the enemy's camp. That in and of itself was enough to warrant another call to Lewis, but he would have to wait. He remained with his back pressed against the wall of the concrete stairwell until the Harley's engine roared again and he could hear the metallic *clank* of the beast switching gears. The bike throttled, a brief low throbbing as the machine turned, its engine a rising growl as it sped past. Barrett peeped up just long enough to confirm that Jackie had boarded and was clinging to the rider's back. They disappeared into the shadows of the darkened town.

What the hell's going on?

Sidling up to the edge and peeking over at the remaining biker kids, Barrett wondered which ones had spray-painted his church and whether or not the Huns had been in on that part of it, too. Was it meant to warn him off? If so, why then? By that point, he had barely gotten involved in all this nonsense. Yet now here he was, embroiled in a biker war and the disappearance of a missing person whose abduction may or may not have been aided and abetted by a bunch of juvenile delinquents. Barrett would just have to follow them, either follow the group or whatever combination of sub-groups or individuals hived off from it. In fact...

Individuals...

If he could get one of those kids alone, he could get him to talk.

Something cold and fierce curled itself inside Barrett's chest like the fingers of a steel fist clenching. He knew it was wrong, of course, to go after kids. But here he was on the outside, without a scrap of useful intel about the situation.

And he was mad.

Barrett was furious that he had become involved in this mess. He was still angry at being beaten up by those kids. He felt powerless and impotent with a lack of information. And he was angry about how this case was bringing up all that stuff *(that piano)* from his childhood, with all the rage and powerlessness it entailed. He felt helpless. He felt like he was drowning.

He would shadow these kids, cut one from the herd and then run him down. Locate the weakest link and pressure him for information. He was resolved to do this thing.

Although he knew it was wrong.

The group was breaking up. Four kids proceeded down an alley behind a building to Barrett's right. Two pedaled down the street beside him, causing him to duck briefly. Two remained talking in the street until parting ways. One, a skinny kid with long hair and a blue backpack, turned down a side street.

Barrett followed him.

———

SUFFER *the little children to come unto me.*

Jesus had most certainly said as much. But the Gospel gave no record of Jesus being stalked by gangs of angry Native teens on bikes who pumped rap music from their belt speakers and beat up passing clergymen. Jesus never taught in an inner-city high-school like the one to which Barrett had been posted briefly as a teacher's aide after ordination, where the bathrooms were warzones and kids dealt each other meth during study hall. Would Jesus suffer the little children to come to Him today? Barrett had his doubts.

So what are you going to do when you get him alone?

He would have to be careful. Assuming he even got a shot at isolating the kid, he would have to do it somewhere that was shielded from view. Someplace that didn't have surveillance cameras. Most places did, these days—even the funeral home. So there was that to consider. Barrett would have to choose his moment carefully.

And how far, Barrett wondered, shivering and pulling his tweed jacket tighter around his shoulders, would he have to go? How much pressure would he have to put on the kid to make him talk?

Jesus. You're talking about a kid, here…

Immediately on the heels of that, a rush of white-hot anger swelled inside him. He was still hopping mad over the beating and wouldn't mind adding a small revenge hit to his quota of sins before he met with the Chief. He could spin it as a mutual attack, depending on how well he hid the act from view.

Jesus, you're talking about lying to the local Natives, roughing up a kid, shielding it from the public eye…

Barrett suddenly felt disgusted with himself. Also a flush of excitement at the notion of revenge. He felt the black tunnel closing around him again—the same one that had closed around him that day with Randy.

God no, don't hurt the kid…

He wouldn't hurt the kid. He commended it into God's hands. Whispered a short but sincere little prayer.

Suppressed his own self-loathing and asked for Grace. Justified it afterwards by reminding himself...

I have no choice.

The kid, meanwhile, had steered back onto the main drag and was angling toward a glowing neon rectangle. Barrett hurried after, recognizing it as the sign of the town's sole fast-food joint, a down-at-heel Hardee's that had opened sometime during the Reagan administration (which also looked to be the last time they'd remodelled the place). Barrett watched the kid pedal up, dismount and lean his bike against the newspaper dispenser. He went inside, the door falling shut behind him, and Barrett double-timed it over, pausing to glance into the lit interior. The place was all but empty. He watched the kid go to the counter, place his order, hand over some money and then make for the bathroom.

Perfect.

Barrett went in after him.

Confidential Informant

"HEY."

Barrett spoke sternly, voice echoing from the windowless tile walls, but inwardly he felt a crumpling of his resolve. As he so often did at moments like this, he suddenly remembered that he had been drinking. And along with that came a sudden awareness of all the limitations, minds and body, drinking imposed on him. *You would think I'd have thought of that beforehand,* he told himself. But he never did. And so had stumbled into some of the biggest catastrophes of his life. He reflected that this could easily become one of them.

Oh, well. In for a penny, in for a pound.

"Hey."

The Native kid kept his back turned as he rubbed his hands beneath the blow dryer. He obviously knew Barrett was there: the priest had seen a swishing of long bangs as the door opened. But since then, he had maintained a preternatural stillness. Barrett imagined the kid living two hundred years ago, squatting in a bush hunting buffalo. Or whatever they hunted out this way. He finished and moved to go around Barrett, head down, but Barrett intercepted, placing a hand on the kid's shoulder and *whap!* It was on.

The punch missed Barrett's temple and ploughed straight into his cheek. Pain exploded below Barrett's eye socket and he grunted, partly in rage, partly in effort as he rotated into the kid, trapping the arm. The kid twisted sideways and tried kicking out clumsily. Barrett mirrored the sideways stance, blocked the kick with a raised knee and then let the kid have it twice in the face with his fist. The kid slipped. Blood sprayed the brown tile wall. Barrett grasped the front of the kid's hoodie, more to haul him upright than to rough him around, but rough him around he did once the kid was back on his feet.

"Listen, I'm *talking* to you. Okay?" Barrett snarled. "You pay *attention* and *answer* me, understand?"

"Answer me, understand?" the kid mocked. Then he giggled and spat. A spot of blood smeared the floor.

"Oh, you're a fucking wise-guy?" Barrett felt suddenly sick. Fought to hold it together. Felt even sicker. "So what were you and your friends doing with Jackie?"

"Who's Jackie?" The kid had stopped fighting and his voice was flat. Dead. Barrett's gut told him the kid really had no clue what Barrett was talking about.

"The girl." Barrett let the kid go but stood, hands on his hips, blocking the kid's way. No mistaking it: he wanted answers. "Jackie is the name of the girl you guys met. But you know her from before."

"No, I *don't*."

"Then *why* did you meet her at the funeral home? You guys met there before."

"No, we *didn't*. I never saw her before. Said she was there to get a lift. A friend was giving her a ride somewhere. That's what she said."

"Why were you there?"

"I dunno.'" The kid shrugged. "I was just bicycling around and I saw everyone there so I went over."

Barrett sighed. The kid knew nothing. But that's when he surprised him with one last nugget.

"She said she was going to meet people at the groundskeeper's place down by the river."

It made sense. Barrett decided to check it out.

"Okay," he told the kid. He released him and began backing out of the bathroom. "We never had this conversation, got it? This never happened. Understand?"

The kid said nothing.

Barrett stepped into the short hallway and almost bumped into the manager.

"What's going on in there?" The manager was a kid of about twenty wearing a shirt and tie, peering through Coke bottle glasses.

"Nothing," muttered Barrett, brushing past him. He heard the bathroom door open and the manager's voice ask the kid if he was alright. But by then Barrett was out the side door and hurrying around the corner of the building to a dark alley, keeping to the shadows.

He had just beaten up *(a child)* a kid. He felt strangely unmoved by it. He might as well have murdered a moth. It was the black tunnel. Always, like this: the tunnel closing around him, shutting out the world, letting him do horrible things. Unspeakable *(Bishop Olmos will recover…)* things, and Olmos wasn't the first.

He put the incident from his mind, focusing on finding the fastest way back to the motel. Within minutes, he was loping back across the lot, fishing the keys to the Hyundai from his pocket as he went. The gold truck was still parked outside the unit beside his. He started up the Hyundai, put in reverse and peeled out, heading for St. Benedict's cemetery.

He followed the meandering road into the dark, remembering his trip out here in daylight. And now, irony of ironies, here was Jackie, years from high-school, once again out rebelling with her friends, taking refuge in her old secret haunts. Barrett wondered if she was thinking about high-school, about her relationship to Mick and the Paladins and the town. She hadn't asked for any of it. She was back out to her old haunts, sure. But now somehow the stakes were higher. Much.

Barrett guided the car down the dirt road toward the trees shrouded in Spanish Moss. He doused the lights and pulled off to the side, a full quarter-mile out from the cemetery. Stepping out, he caught sight of a glimmer in the trees ahead, heard the tinny sound of rock music on a transistor radio. Using his cell-phone, he was able to throw a small globe of light into the black. He followed it, stepping carefully along the rutted track, ducking under the moss-laden tree where he'd parked on his first visit, sneaking down the path to a point close to the groundskeeper's shed.

Barrett counted five Harleys, their chrome gleaming in the light of a campfire. Huns lounged on makeshift furniture—crates, boulders, blankets laid down in the grass. The radio sat on a nearby picnic table, tuned to an oldies station. A Grateful Dead song oiled out of the speakers. Barrett was trying to remember its name when he caught sight of Jackie. It was, he realized, the first time he had ever seen her smile. She was curled around the lanky form of a blond, skinny Hun who held court from the saddle of his bike, the one parked nearest the firepit. He was telling a story—either that or an elaborate joke. The other Huns were laughing and so was Jackie, taking swigs from the beer can she occasionally stole from his grasp. Barrett recognized genuine happiness when he saw it. Jackie and her biker beau displayed all the hallmarks of two people were incurably in love. The contrast between her expression when she had been with Randy and her expression now could not have been more different.

So she's dating a Hun. Barrett wondered how Big Mick would feel about something like that. Probably not good.

It occurred to Barrett that perhaps he had been wrong about the Indian kids having anything to do with Randy's body. Or Jackie for that matter. And his mind went back to that bathroom and what he had done to that kid and it suddenly occurred to him that he might have beaten the shit out of a perfectly innocent person. He felt terrible but then reminded himself that he had been drinking. And along with that came an awareness of all the limitations drinking imposed on him, mind and body. *What didn't I think of that before?* Barrett shook his head…

No.

For not the first time in his life, he considered quitting. This wasn't his first major stumble while on booze. And, if he kept drinking, it wouldn't be the last. As always when he began to question his need to drink, Barrett shut down the line of thought brutally:

If anyone is entitled to, I am.

And with that thought came an implosion of sadness in his chest.

He knew he *could* live without booze. If he had a

reason to.

As if to prove to himself that booze didn't impair him that much, he crept away in perfect, textbook silence. He drove back into town feeling an inner chill that was colder than the grave.

————

HE WASN'T TOO late for the liquor store.

"Any sign of those Indian kids?" he asked, paying for a box of wine.

"No sign of them." She made change. "Been awful quiet around here. Been kinda' nice, I won't lie. Man!"

He made his way slowly back to the motel. Pulling into the lot, he noted Lewis' Crown Victoria parked in front of his unit. The gold pick-up truck was gone. Barrett parked and stepped out.

"Evening, padre." Lewis slid from the driver's seat and would not meet Barrett's eye. "Padre, how much have you had to drink tonight?"

"I, uh, lost count. A while back."

"Uh-huh." Lewis was looking at him now, head tilted back, staring down the length of his nose at the priest. "Padre, there's no easy way to say this. I'm here to take you into custody. You're under arrest."

Barrett sighed. "Okay. But you should know…the kid hit me first."

"*Hit* you?" Lewis frowned. "What are you talking about?"

"What are *you* talking about?"

But by then Lewis was walking around the side of the car, tugging his handcuffs out of his belt. "I'm talking about what happened in the bathroom at Hardee's. Father, you're under arrest for sexual interference with a minor, inappropriate touching, and invitation to sexual activity. That's the charge. Now turn around and put your hands behind your back."

Pedomania

"O...KAY." Ann Fletcher, Esquire, sighed and pushed her eyeglasses up into her salt-and-pepper bangs. Barrett remembered the gesture from last time. But gone were the glances of near-pity. Instead, she looked worried and more than a little pissed off as she closed the file folder containing the police report. She leaned across the table of the small interview room Walton had shown them into for the purpose of this meeting. "So. Just tell me what happened."

"I...beat the kid up. He wouldn't answer my question."

"What question?"

"That's, ah, personal..."

"Well, it *can't* be personal, Father Barrett. Let me tell you why. Because if your question was *'will you suck my dick?'* that's going to pose a whole different set of problems from what might arise if our question was, for example, *'have you tried the Hardee's Supreme-o?'* You catch my drift? This is like the confessional. Everything you say is confidential but you can't keep any secrets from me. This is how it works. Otherwise, you better get yourself another lawyer."

"But you're the only lawyer in this town."

"I know." She smiled. "It's great, isn't it? For me, it truly is a seller's market. But back to your problem. Had you been drinking? Actually, let me rephrase…How *much* had you been drinking?"

"Oh, the usual amount…"

"Okay. We'll say '*a lot.*'" She took up a pencil. "So you followed the kid into the bathroom to ask him your question. So it's something private. What is it?"

"I'm…looking into something. Sort of as a favor. To a friend."

"Like an investigation?"

"Something like that."

"Alright, so what was the question?"

"It pertains to a missing person."

Ann Fletcher, Esquire frowned. "Are the police involved?"

"I expect so."

"Who?"

"I can't say."

"And you're looking into this…why?"

"For a parishioner."

"Okay. Fair enough. That I can take to a judge. But this beating you gave the kid…"

"I thought this was a case about pedophilia."

"Yes, but the beating is going to come up." She threw down her pencil. "Why, Barrett? What possessed you to beat up a child? Why the hell would anyone *do* that? Was it the booze?"

"Partly."

"Okay, so what else? What makes you so fucked up?"

Barrett was silent for a long time. Impatience gathered like a storm on Ann Fletcher, Esquire's, face and, after a certain point, she opened her mouth to speak. But he beat her to it.

"My dad was somebody important in his world." Barrett shifted uncomfortably. "I don't know much about his world. Not as much as you might imagine but it was a world where power and weakness couldn't co-exist. I knew my father was a dangerous man. The way you know a dog is dangerous without even hearing it growl. Animals like that carry a sense of their own danger around with them for everyone to feel. And I could feel it on my dad. So could a lot of people. It was the secret to his success.

"My father's professional life and our personal lives were mixed. There were a lot of gatherings at the house. I remember them as a kid. I used to hide under the piano." Again, the pained smile. "I spent a lot of time as a kid wanting to be invisible. And I achieved it. Learned to behave like a piece of the décor. I could be in a room standing right out in the open and nobody would even notice I was there. That's what it took for me to survive in my father's world. Because there were times I wasn't *supposed* to be there. But I could never tell in advance when that would be so I learned to be there and not there.

"One night, when I was six, when I was there and not there, I was lying under the piano. I stayed for a long time. There was a party, you see. What they used to call a 'cocktail party.' I don't know if people still have those but my parents used to have them all the time. I would be under the piano and could see all the legs and shoes of the people attending. Anyway, this one night I think I must have fallen asleep because when I woke up it was dark and there were only two people in the room—my dad and another man.

"My dad was talking. It was low. Difficult to hear. But you could tell by the feeling in the room that something wasn't right. The other man would start to talk and silence would fall. And then he would fall into the silence. It was like he couldn't complete a sentence. It was during one of those silences that dad shot him."

Ann Fletcher, Esquire, stopped breathing.

"I didn't understand at first but I figured it out pretty quick. There was this muffled *bang!* and then the other man was falling. He dropped right beside the piano, his face turned toward me, his hands up to cover this red mess spreading on his shirt. He wasn't quite dead when he hit the floor. Soon, the red mess spilled out from behind his hands. I know he saw me. I saw him seeing me. And I was scared he would tell my dad I was hiding there. But in the end I didn't have to worry because he died. Right there in front of me. I watched his breathing stop and the light fade from his eyes. Then my dad left the room and made a phone call.

"Some men came and removed the body. By then I had slipped out from under the piano and back down the hall to my room. I watched them carry out something draped in a canvas tarp. Then my father fixed himself a drink and sat down at the piano. He played rather well. Gershwin. 'Rhapsody in Blue.' Then he finished his drink and went to bed."

Ann Fletcher, Esquire sat very still, one finger in front of her mouth, her other arm over the back of her chair. She watched Barrett with the careful patience of a hunting wolf. And when she spoke it was very gently, as she might speak to a very frightened child.

"I'm going to…speak to Crown. And I'm going to

ask that you sit down with a psychiatrist. Not on a long-term basis. Just something I can show the judge."

"Something that says what?"

"You want the truth, Barrett?" She stood and jammed her notepad into her document case. "You're an absolute mess. A terminal alcoholic with a penchant for violence—a priest with a *police* record, for god's sake. You've been removed from parish duties. And you've just been arrested for *beating up a child.* I'm no shrink, but you're the psychological equivalent of Afghanistan. Given what you've told me just now about your past and a favorable evaluation from a psychologist, I'm pretty sure I can get you released on a psychiatric exemption. You'll have to go through treatment. And enough AA meetings to convince them you're at least trying not to kill yourself with booze. But I'm fairly confident I can get that deal for you. We'll see what the tribe decides to do. But if charges go forward, that'll be our strategy."

Barrett thought for a minute. "Okay," he said at last.

Nodding, she made for the interrogation room door. She raised her hand to knock, then paused. She turned to him.

"Barrett, for what it's worth, I don't think you should kill yourself. I think you should find some way to live. Something to live *for.* I'd think already having such a reason would be a prerequisite in your line of work, but sometimes people fake it until they make it. Stop drinking long enough to take a look in the mirror and take stock of what's left before it's too late."

She knocked twice and Walton let her out. A minute later, Lewis stepped in.

"Well, you're bailed and free to go. They're not pressing charges."

"Wait. Someone paid—"

Lewis nodded. "They're outside."

When Barrett stepped onto the sidewalk, he was surprised to find it empty. There was no one there except some old Indian guy who—

"Hello."

—who wore a green baseball cap, and...

Some old fat guy in a green baseball cap showed up. Native. Didn't hear what he said, but he talked to them real quiet-like for about ten seconds. Then they all mounted up and followed him..."

"Hi." Barrett was caught off guard. "I, I've...heard about you."

"I expect so." The old man smiled sadly. "I'm the local Chief. Those boys, the ones who beat you up, they're from our band. They're sorry they done it. We're taking care of it."

"I...well. Thank you."

"We figure they beat you up, you beat up Johnny. Fair is fair. We don't want no trouble with the church, and besides, Johnny can be a little asshole sometimes. I get it." The Chief chose his next words carefully. "We don't believe you're a pedophile. Johnny admitted to making that part up. But it's a good thing because it gives us a chance to talk."

"Did you—"

"Did I what?"

"Did you just bail me out?"

"Yep. I expect I've paid for Lewis and Walton's next hunting trip, licenses, and ammo. Maybe even a new tent." The Chief laughed and shook his head. "That Gavin's a real old coyote, he is."

Barrett, mind reeling, managed to stay upright. This wasn't just the usual morning hangover bedevilling him. For the life of him, Barrett couldn't imagine bailing out someone suspected of molesting a child, especially someone who might have harmed a parish child. The fact that the Chief had done so was an act of utmost charity. '*Christian' charity,* Barrett corrected himself. What had Ann Fletcher, Esquire, said about having something to live for? He suddenly felt very small.

"In the old times, we would have just ridden over to your place and, I dunno', done something violent." The Chief's gaze was uncomfortably frank. "There's some men in the tribe want to kick your ass, I'll be honest, but that won't happen. You were wronged and you lashed out. Now it's over. That's the first thing. The boys who hurt you are going into the longhouse for a while. They'll answer for what they did. So from our point-of-view, this thing is over between you. Is that how you see it, Father Barrett?"

"Yes. Yes, I do."

The Chief nodded. "So we're agreed on that. I'm glad. You might ask yourself what you can do for Johnny and his family. Praying for them might be a good start. His sister is pregnant. She turns seventeen next month."

Barrett said nothing.

"Gavin talked to me about what happened to Scooter. He's a good old guy, is Scooter. Always been kind to us."

"What…Chief, what is your tribe called?"

"You couldn't pronounce it. It's a long Indian word that translates to 'People of the Otter.'"

Barrett smiled. "I'll remember."

"Some of the grandmothers will be stopping by Scooter's place later. They heard he got beat up and they baked up a storm." The Chief chuckled. "I hope he likes flat bread."

"I'm sure he'll be grateful."

The Chief was nodding. "We spoke to the boys about Scooter, me and the Elders. Father, they said they didn't attack him and I believe them. Just doesn't make any sense."

"Well, he said he interrupted them while they were spray-painting the church…"

"No." The Chief's voice was firm. "They say they didn't beat up Scooter and I believe them. And as for vandalizing your church? Father, I'm very sorry that happened. But our kids didn't do it. We raised them better than that. They didn't vandalize your church. No Indian person would do that."

Audience

HE WAS CLIMBING out from under the piano.

It wasn't easy. First he was six and then suddenly he was seventeen. Then he kept switching back and forth between bodies, which made it difficult for him to coordinate his movements and make headway. Also, the corpse on the floor beside him kept changing. One moment, it was the dying man his father shot and then it was his mother. It was creepy and unsettling but he was making progress, clambering out and reaching toward a window filled with sunlight. Then the sunlight was covered by a mantle of clouds and thunder hammered the sky which became the pounding on his motel room door that awakened him.

Barrett rolled from bed and stumbled across the carpet to grasp the knob and wrench it open.

"Father." One of the Paladins, a young guy, looked panicked. "Big Mick sent me. You've got to come right away."

"Why? What's going on?" Barrett rubbed his head and did his best to focus on the kid.

"Hurry up and get dressed." The kid was insistent but nervous. "C'mon, father. Hurry up. It's a matter of life and death."

———

BIG MICK'S compound looked different in full daylight: smaller, seedier, more wreckage-strewn and disorganized than Barrett remembered. Darkness apparently concealed a multitude of blemishes. The kid navigated his Harley up to the open garage door and braked to a stop.

"Mick and Pappy are inside, father." The kid indicated the door with a jerk of his chin. "They're waiting for you."

Barrett dismounted and ducked below the partially-closed door to enter the space where he'd first met the Paladins. Like last time, the bikers were scattered across the floor and furniture of the make-shift living room. But the beer cups and kegs had been replaced by stacks of ammo and the glint of blued steel. The Paladins were variously occupied cleaning and loading an array of firearms. The room bristled with weaponry. A sense of menace hung in the air.

"Hey, father." Mick put aside the assault rifle he had been polishing and rose to shake Barrett's hand. "Word got back to me you were asking around about Jackie. Thank you. That's right nice of you, father."

"Sure is, father," Pappy chimed in, looking up from loading the shotgun broken open over his knee. "We appreciate it."

Barrett started to sweat slightly. "Well, yeah. Sure. As long as you guys don't mind. I was just concerned, so…"

"Nah." Big Mick was flapping a hand. "We appre-

ciate it. We really do. That's why we asked you out here."
He smirked. "Wanted to know what you'd found out."

Barrett smiled. *Oh shit.* "Sure. Well, first of all…the
people I spoke to are very concerned for Jackie's
welfare…"

"Oh? Why's that? Because we haven't shared
anything with anyone. We're keeping this all right in the
family, aren't we, Pappy?"

"Sure are, Mick." Pappy was staring at Barrett now.
So were a few other Paladins.

"Oh, no…" Barrett flapped a hand, thinking fast.
"Of course. But you should know that Lewis, the RCMP
guy, he's a little suspicious. And *he* actually approached
me and asked how everything was with Jackie because
he'd noticed she wasn't hanging around her usual
haunts."

At this, Mick and Pappy were surprised.

"Lewis is a cagey one." Barrett raised his eyebrows
and showed his palms—signs of absolute openness ('submission' they call it in interviewing and interrogation).
Because now he had veered into the truth, something he
could discuss comfortably. "He's even hip to the fact that
I've been replaced at the parish and I haven't talked
about that with anybody."

"You leaving, father?" Mick sounded concerned.

"Well…no." Barrett shrugged. "I'm on suspension
with pay right now. Which is kind of why I have all this
spare time to poke around and ask questions. The Archbishop wants me to stick around because I guess he
doesn't have a lot of confidence in the new priest, a guy
named Father—"

"You mean Father Dolan?" Mick snickered as he
spoke.

"Dolan?" Pappy's expression was sour. "He's always

looking to rent U-Hauls from us down at the yard. That guy's got a *lot* of stuff he packs around!"

"He's a hoarder," Barrett affirmed.

"That explains a lot," muttered Pappy, returning his attention to the shotgun. Barrett seized the initiative.

"So, I told Lewis that Jackie was one of a handful of young people I know from around town who I keep an eye on."

Now Big Mick was nodding. "Smart. That's good, father. Thanks."

"Oh, of course. I mean, I have the seal of the confessional to consider. Anything we discuss is confidential."

"The church is a law unto itself." Pappy had put aside the shotgun and had picked up an automatic pistol—a Colt .45—from the table beside him. "Priests are like bikers that way, Mick. They have a Code. Same as us. And they keep things in the family. Which is actually something I was curious about, father."

"Oh?"

"Yeah." Pappy took up a rag and wiped down the pistol as he talked. "How do you keep order among priests? How do you maintain justice?"

"Well…" Barrett shifted uncomfortably. "You have other priests. Investigators. I was one, in fact. Our job was to make sure other priests followed the rules."

"So, you were the law for a church that's a law unto itself."

"Yeah."

Pappy laughed. "Talk about being an outsider."

"Yeah." Mick interposed. "But talk about having a lot of power."

"Judge and jury," Pappy said.

Minister and executioner, thought Barrett. That was the position in which he now found himself. The secrets of Fulton had coalesced around him powerfully enough to create a church all their own. Given that he was becoming the unofficial chaplain to a gang of outlaw bikers, perhaps that church was his true parish now.

"Do you remember when Jackie was in high-school?" he asked.

Mick, who was hunched forward, sat up straight at this. "Sure. Yeah, she was a handful. Why?"

"Did she ever tell you about…the house by the river? The cemetery?"

"No." Mick's eyes narrowed and the tone in which he spoke was sharp. Now he and Pappy and everyone in the garage was watching Barrett. "Why?"

Barrett swallowed. "Okay. Apparently she used to hang out around there in high-school. I found out from my groundskeeper, Scooter. He knew Jackie back then. He used to be—"

"Janitor at the school. Yeah." Mick smiled. "I know Scooter. He's alright."

"There's an abandoned groundskeeper's building at the old Anglican cemetery by the river. Jackie and her friends—along with every other high-school kid in a hundred-mile radius, I'd guess—liked to squat there and party."

"Really." Mick's face spread in a slow smile.

"I went and investigated. I found indications that the place had been recently—"

"That's where the Huns are massing." Pappy's voice was steely. "We reconnoitered out that way this morning and found the remains of their camp."

"We're going back." Mick grabbed an Uzi machine-pistol up from the workbench beside him. "We're going to finish this."

"Finish what?" Barrett's voice rose in panic. "Jesus, man. What are you planning to do?"

"We're going to fucking kill the lot of them, father. End this war. Take their territory and add it to ours. That's how this works."

"Violence begets violence."

"Basically yeah." Mick smiled frostily.

"Okay, look." Barrett held up his hands. "What if I could get them to leave peacefully? Let me go in there and parley and use that time to see if Jackie's taken up with them. That's what you accused them of that afternoon at the Junction, right? Let's see if it's true. I mean, you wouldn't want to go in there, great guns blazing, if there's a possibility she's inside, would you?"

"With a Hun war party?" Pappy shook his head. "Sorry, padre, but her hanging with that group don't seem too likely to me…"

"Nevertheless. Don't you think we should make sure?"

"Yeah." Big Mick was cradling the Uzi, looking pensively at the floor. "No, you're right, father. It's a good plan. Plus you can bring us back some intel on their strength, the kind of weapons they got, all that stuff. I'll hold off until midnight. If I don't hear from you by then, we're going in."

"Certainly." Barrett hated himself for agreeing but did so all the same.

"I'll send a few of the boys along with you…"

"Actually, no…" Barrett thought for a moment. "I have somebody I'd rather bring along with me for a job like this."

For a moment, Mick looked confused. "Why?"

Barrett thought for a moment. "I suppose it's like you said. Sometimes you meet people who do something for you. And you greet that blessing with a request for them to do one thing more."

Mick shrugged. "Suit yourself."

Barrett checked his watch.

9 AM.

He had until midnight to stop a war.

Motive

"THIS IS A HANDY LITTLE BOAT," said the Chief, navigating the shoals by feel. The moon was high, the night was chilly and the outboard purred along, the river unspooling beneath them on a carpet of shimmering silver.

"I didn't know your people *had* boats."

"Well, what do you expect?" The Chief threw Barrett a sour look. "We're called the People of the Otter, for goodness sake. You think we wouldn't have boats?"

"Well, now that you mention it, most of the natives I've met around here travel by bicycle…"

"That's what killed us, you know," the Chief deadpanned. "When Columbus came. It was the bicycle gap. If we'd had ten speeds, we would have sent that jamoke packing back to Spain where he belonged."

"Wise guy, huh?"

"Takes wisdom to be a real live Indian Chief."

They came to a bend in the river where a grassy peninsula jutted into the waters, forcing a course change.

The Chief steered around the headland and then cut the motor.

"What now?" asked Barrett.

"Go ahead and position those oars for me. The ones there on the deck."

Barrett looked down at the deck between his feet. A pair of thick, industrial strength oars were slotted into their storage grooves. It took some doing, but Barrett managed to unfasten and then lift them one at a time. The heavy metal pins settled into the thick oar locks. When he was done and both oars were set, his shoulders ached and he was panting.

"Okay. Next?"

"Start rowing." The Chief settled back and clasped his hands behind his head, staring out at the river. "It's a nice night to go for a paddle on this river."

Barrett clenched his jaw but said nothing. Settling himself amidships, he grasped an oars in each hand, leaned forward, dipped and stroked. The oars bit and the boat shifted briefly onto the diagonal before Barrett brought it true in the current. He leaned forward again and pulled. Bent, dipped and stroked. They were running with the current, parallel to shore. Barrett could hear his own breathing, the plash and squeak of the oars as he rowed. Then another sound cut in: the dim clamour of a radio in the middle distance.

"Pull in there." The Chief pointed. "That little stone beach with the tree."

Barrett saw. It didn't take much to put the boat around and pull for shore. The Chief jumped in where the tide was knee-deep and pulled them onto the shingle.

"We're here." He grabbed the line and looped it around the thin bole of the short tree on the beach.

"Head up this bank and the groundkeeper's place is about five hundred yards away through the trees."

"You're sure?"

"My scouts can tell us." The Chief grinned and led the way up the slope. Barrett followed. At the top, shrouded in shadows, they waited. After a minute, they could hear the ticking of bicycle wheels approaching. Two kids in black hoodies materialized out of the foliage astride their street bikes. The Chief whispered to them in their native tongue and they pedaled over.

"How is everything?" the Chief asked.

"There's a lot of them," said one boy, a stout kid with buck teeth. "Probably thirty. All with their motorcycles."

"They got guns?" asked the Chief.

The two boys traded a look before nodding emphatically.

The Chief turned to Barrett. "Be careful."

"I will." Barrett glanced at the boys. "Thank you, guys."

"You're welcome," said the buck-toothed one. Then he and his partner dismounted and began lowering their bikes down the slope toward the boat. It wasn't until they were lifting them aboard that Barrett realized the other boy was Johnny, the kid he had punched out. Johnny lifted and handed his partner's bike to him, then pushed the boat out from the beach into the current. Together, he and his buck-tooth pal unshipped the oars and began maneuvering back the way they'd come.

Overcome by a spasm of fatigue, Barrett closed his eyes. Swayed briefly on his heels. Tired. God he was so tired. And…

He was alone.

This is what it was, he reflected, to be a priest. Because to be a priest was, by definition, to walk alone with only God for company. Let the Lutherans and the Episcopalians and the Baptists have their wives. To be a follower of the Throne of Peter was to forsake all such worldly companionship. In Barrett's case, he had been alone his whole life so it had been an easy fit. But the aloneness, the isolation, the moving from town to town…It was all starting to bear down on him like a load of rocks. And he was tired.

So tired.

He produced his cell phone and switched on the flashlight app. He listened again for the radio then bent his steps in that direction. The hubbub of voices grew. It was a sizeable crowd and, obvious as he approached it through the trees, a lively one. A huge pile of logs burned in the fire pit and as Barrett approached, a man took a running leap and managed to clear the pit, beer in hand, to the whooping and cheering of his mates. Barrett switched off the flashlight and pocketed his cell phone. He paused just outside the firelight, his priestly garb keeping him hidden in the shadows as he scanned for Jackie. He didn't see her, but a sense of her presence lingered around the campfire like musk. He also didn't see the lanky blond biker in whose arms she'd found refuge. No sign of them, but Jackie was obviously involved, and deeply, with a member of the opposing camp. This was no summer romance—this was love. Barrett snorted.

Women!

He remained motionless, just outside the flickering glow, until someone noticed him.

"Hey!" Hunter, the bald, sinewy Hun with the nose-ring whom Mick had threatened at the bar, whirled and came to his feet. "The fuck?"

"Hello." Barrett offered a neutral smile. "Mind if I join you?"

Hunter dashed his beer can to the ground, stormed over to Barrett and dragged him back into the firelight by his lapels.

"What the fuck you doing here, father?" Hunter shook him. "You got a death wish, sneaking up on a camp of Huns in the middle of the night?"

"It's not that late yet, is it?" Barrett waited until Hunter paused shaking him to glance at his watch. It was ten-forty PM.

"What do you *want?*" On the last world, Hunter launched Barrett across the grass to fall in a heap by the edge of the firepit. Hoots of laughter swirled as he grappled himself upright, brushing grass from his jacket.

"Listen, guys…" Barrett suppressed the urge to break Hunter's jaw. "I'm here as a priest. I'm on an errand of mercy. A young woman has gone missing from our community and I'm concerned—"

"Concerned?" Hunter guffawed. He clawed a fresh beer loose from a cooler and ripped off the tab. "*You?* I've heard about you. Father Barrett. The fucking drunk priest who beats up kids. Didn't you get busted? Put on the bench from parish priest for that? Or was it somebody else you beat up? You're a fucking loser and a drunk. You don't give a shit about anybody but yourself. Here." Hunter jammed the can into Barrett's hand. "Have a drink and come back down to Earth, father. Because nobody's buying your guardian angel rap."

A sandstorm scoured Barrett's insides. He didn't like being forced to pay attention to home truths about himself. He liked hearing about them from other people even less. But it was true. Everything Hunter had said was true. Totally, unqualifiedly and undeniably true. He was a fucking loser and a drunk. Being an alcoholic meant he screwed up regularly. Made bad choices. Got violent. Ruined one career, then another. And felt free to behave that way and make those choices because he didn't think he was ever hurting anyone but himself. His life was so remote, so isolated, so insignificant that none of his choices mattered…

But somehow this mattered. *Jackie* mattered.

She was every kid he was too late to save. She was every angel from his past who found a better future. He needed to find her. Because if she could disappear and be dragged into a biker war, then anyone in Fulton could. And even if they weren't all Catholic, they were—in a very real sense—under his pastoral care. Much more so than under the care of that nincompoop Dolan. Barrett suddenly realized he wasn't alone. That he had a responsibility. And he was going to see it through this time.

"That's as may be." He was speaking, the black tunnel around him now, the words coming from somewhere else. "But you see I'm not leaving here until I have some idea what's going on with Jackie. And I think you're the man to tell me, Hunter. Because this is your crew and probably very little of what happens among them happens without your noticing. So help me out. And let me help you out. Just tell me where Jackie is."

"Help *me* out?" Hunter laughed. "How you planning on doing that, pops? You don't have anything I want. Hell, you don't even *know* what I want."

"Actually, I think I do." Barrett smiled tiredly. "You came into town, great guns blazing, all set for a showdown and then things went sideways. You had to retreat and regroup. That's why you've been sending advance units of riders out here to stake out this place and keep an eye on things in town. My guess is you've decided the game isn't worth the candle. You're not going to come in and take territory. Too big a bite for you. But you had to come out here yourself one last time. Party and spend the night here to show everybody you're not afraid. And then a final loud, blasting blow-out ride through town. That's probably the plan, right?"

Hunter stood, face white, eyes wide with rage, lips pressed tightly together. He was right on the edge of blowing when Barrett added:

"That's never going to happen because the Paladins are planning to hit you tonight. And unless you tell me where Jackie is, this won't end for you. The Paladins will start raiding Hun territory. One ride-through, one drive-by at a time, but it will happen. And when your strength is cut, they'll come after you. I have to be able to prove to Mick that you bargained the life of his daughter in good faith. Then he'll let you live. Anything less and he'll kill you."

Hunter and his main guys were trading glances. Even without lifting a finger, Barrett could see, Hunter was giving orders. A few guys moved off and began packing up the beer and camping stuff, getting ready to ride out.

"Jackie fell in with Deke." Hunter's voice was tired, husky. He'd had enough of drama. "His brother's got a place here. Not sure where. It's a mobile home, that much I know. Guy drives a gold—"

"A gold pick-up truck." Barrett slammed his open palm with a fist. "You betchya."

He turned to go.

"Hey, padre."

Barrett turned back.

"You got some balls for a priest, man." Hunter's tone was one of genuine approval. "Takes a lot of guts to walk into the middle of a bunch of bikers without a gun."

Barrett spread his arms. "What makes you so sure I don't have one?"

"Doesn't that go against your priestly vows or whatever?"

Barrett laughed. "Even Jesus broke the rules from time to time."

Seeing Is Believing

"MICK."

"Father? It's…" A pause. "Eleven-twenty. We were just on our way out the door."

"Stay put. Jackie's safe. I'm bringing her home tomorrow."

"Where is she?"

"She's safe. Look…Call off the raid. Hunter and his boys are going home."

Another long pause. Then: "What time will you bring her back tomorrow?"

"As early as I can. Just stay where you are. Open a few beers. Relax. This is almost over."

———

IN FULTON, all roads lead to McLellan's.

McLellan's started life as a supermarket back in the late 1950s, only to be purchased and sectioned into separate retail establishments in the mid-1960s. It lay dormant in the Seventies and Eighties until Arnold

McLellan purchased it in 1992 and began knocking down walls. Although never fully reintegrated back into its pristine, single showroom state, McLellan's was a more or less open space into which a half-dozen separate retail pipelines spilled. At McLellan's, one could buy groceries, clothing or hardware items. A bookstore/coffee shop did brisk business near the wide foyer with two storefronts, through which rotated a succession of seasonal and/or short-lived businesses. At the moment, one was empty while the other housed an H&R Block outlet.

Barrett limped in past the rampant bear wearing the hockey jersey and made for the back of the store. Coming to an anonymous steel door with a peep-hole, he knocked. It was opened by a clean-cut young man wearing a Lacoste shirt whose hair was cut in a new crew cut.

"Father Barrett! How are you?"

"Just fine, Homer. I need your help."

"You got it, father. Come in." Homer Anderson, McLellan's store detective, led Barrett into a narrow windowless office dominated by four large CCTV monitors and invited him to sit in one of the two padded leather chairs. Barrett settled in with a groan.

"How's your mom?" He rubbed his eyes. Dragged his fingers through his hair, pulling at his scalp to keep himself focused.

"She's fine, father." Homer sounded relieved. "The operation went well. We should be back at church this Sunday. We missed you Sunday! For some reason, Father Dolan did the service."

"He's helping out," Barrett said diplomatically. "Taking on some of my duties so I can handle a few things around the parish. That's actually why I'm here."

"How can I help?"

Barrett produced and unfolded a scrap of paper from his pocket. "I'm trying to track down the daughter of a friend. I'm thinking the chances are pretty good she would have come in here last…Thursday." Barrett consulted the paper and thought back. Friday had been the day the Huns rolled into town—the day after he'd found the graffiti on the side of the church. "Apparently she's been spotted getting in and out of a gold pick-up truck. You have exterior cameras?"

"Sure do, father." Homer leaned forward and began tapping on the keyboard. "Thursday you say? That's usually a pretty busy time…"

"I know it. If we could look at some CCTV. Say starting around ten AM or thereabouts. Say, main entrance and parking lot."

Ordinarily, CCTV footage was available only to cops and store management. But Homer was a good Catholic boy. He brought up the main entrance camera. As it happened, the video timer was positioned for 0945. He hit play and the forms of shoppers, as seen from above and at a slight angle, filled the screen, blasting details at the viewer in close-up. The shot was focused such that you had a clear shot of a customer's face for their first two or three seconds in the breezeway and then a really good look at their apparel from the neck down as they walked out of the shot and into the store. Barrett appreciated Homer's choosing the best angles from which to capture still shots for the police.

Homer bumped the film up to one-and-a-quarter speed. Jackie walked into the shot at 0958 hours.

"Okay stop there."

"Let me get you faces first." Homer's fingers flew over his keyboard and mouse. The shot enlarged, rewound, its focus filter adjusted and then replayed. Jackie walked in beside the lanky, blond biker Barrett had seen her with the first night at the groundkeeper's cottage. A few seconds behind them came a third figure. At first, he seemed separate from the couple but then the male turned and spoke to him.

"You want the couple first or…"

"The guy behind."

Homer worked his magic. The third man's face leapt onscreen, frozen facing the camera. He was olive-skinned, balding and had a thick gold hoop in his left ear. To Barrett he looked like a cross between an Elizabethan sailor and the owner of a Turkish brothel. Barrett mentally nicknamed him the Gigolo.

"Looks like they were headed straight down the main aisle." Homer switched cameras. In the middle-distance, the trio turned in the empty space by the cash registers, choosing a direction. A fourth person walked behind them into the store—a ponderous, slow-moving figure that Barrett sensed he knew but could not place. He passed Jackie and friends and went down a narrow aisle. After a moment, the trio followed him.

"Hardware aisle." Homer switched cameras again and Jackie and friends walked right into the shot. They were checking out a selection of duct tape on the shelf. The man whom they'd followed was further down, his back to the camera.

I know him, Barrett thought. *But* who *is it?*

"Okay, father. They've grabbed two packs of Gorilla tape and looks like they're headed up to the front. We can check the parking lot to see what vehicle they get into."

"It will be a gold pick-up," muttered Barrett. His voice was muted and he wore a stunned expression.

Because he had finally recognized the figure in the hardware aisle.

Barrett couldn't possibly imagine why he was there or what he could possibly need. Because God knew, he had enough stuff already. Enough to fill entire rooms. And when Barrett saw the item he draped over his arm from a bin after selecting two cans of spray-paint, he began to quiver with rage.

―――――

"YEAH," Lewis was saying, "I did a string search on that partial license plate. Found a gold pick-up truck. It's registered in YouBou but the local address is on Crowley Street."

"Perfect." Barrett slid into the Hyundai and spun the ignition. "Thanks for checking. I'll repay it with a treat. I've got good news." Barrett slid the car into gear and pulled away from the curb.

"Oh? What's that?"

"The Huns are leaving."

"Didn't know they were here."

"They've been camping out at that groundskeeper's place by St. Benedict's, the old Anglican cemetery. Advance parties. I guess they've been planning to stage a raid on the Paladins' club-house and absorb Fulton into their territory."

"I see! You *are* well-informed…"

"I have a confidential informant." *Had,* Barrett thought, turning toward the neighborhood Lewis had mentioned. "Anyway, they've given up on the idea. Decided to pack it up and go home. You might want to keep an eye peeled on the highway. Make sure they get underway safely."

"Will do. Thanks. The more distance they put between themselves and Mick's goons, the better. Speaking of which… Where are you headed?"

"I'm off to finish this. Expect a call in an hour."

"Will do. Be safe." Lewis clicked off.

───────

CROWLEY STREET: even Barrett knew the name. It was Fulton's seediest neighborhood—a jumble of strip-joints, diners and garages that bled into the highway on the north end of town. All of the above plus one trailer park. Barrett steered in that direction and floored it.

The main drag ended and he twisted the wheel, scooting down Avro Lane. The intersection to Crowley Street loomed ahead. Barrett took a left and spotted the park almost immediately, its entrance fronted by a huge green sign: *LILAC ACRES*. It seemed to Barrett a funny name for a place sandwiched between a lumber yard and a trucking company. He turned in and began cruising up and down the aisles of campers, fifth wheels and mobile homes, searching.

Depressing wasn't even the right word for the place. People ended up living in trailer parks for all sorts of reasons, but the baseline similarity seemed to be the bad breaks. Whether born into poverty or being proud owner of a history of bad choices, ending up down-and-out, lost, addicted all led to places like this, Barrett thought as he examined the worn siding and rusty TV antennas of the passing trailers. Every now and then, somebody made an attempt to prettify their lot with a picket fence or a fancy carport tent, but for the most part it was row after row of depressing, bleak, dead-end RV housing.

He spotted the gold pick-up parked in the driveway

of a lot occupied by an old silver Air Stream camper trailer, one of those with an exterior of burnished silver. The blinds were drawn and the doors of the Air Stream were closed. A handful of Harleys, Barrett saw, were parked in the shade on its far side. Just a handful.

So the Gigolo has some friends visiting. Barrett drove back to visitor parking and found a spot. *Five will get you ten they're Huns.*

He sat in the driver's seat for a few minutes, gazing out at the silent park. He recalled being in similar situations on the force in Toronto, rolling up on some house where there was trouble, either a domestic violence incident or some suspect barricaded within. Back in those days, he would park and wait for back-up—another uniform to cover his six during the door-knock. But these days he was wearing a different uniform—one from a very different organization with a different command structure and a very different kind of back-up.

Find some way to live…something to live for…

Ann Fletcher's words collided with his thoughts, bumping them into an entirely different direction. The uniform he now wore presupposed (hell, advertised!) that he had faith. But faced with the prospect of walking into a potentially violent situation, Barrett felt foolish reaching out in prayer. And the fact that he did made him feel uneasy about himself.

Why are you doing this, then?

His family had failed him. His friends had failed him. His career and the law had failed him. The church had failed him. Expecting each of them to be there when he stumbled, Barrett had instead been disappointed when they had all punished him for his circumstances, his failures, his weaknesses, his lapses in judgment. All had forsaken him the moment it became inconvenient to support him.

So what did that leave?

Doing the right thing. A fist closed inside Barrett's chest. *A missing girl and a father who's worried. A biker war on the edge of blowing up. A town hanging in the balance. Somebody has to step up.*

Barrett was ready to do so. But he wasn't sure why. Anguish flooded him and he bent his forehead to the steering wheel.

My God, why have you forsaken me?

It was like Bishop Olmos and his flock of pedo priests. Someone had to take action. Because someone had to do something. Because men had to be seen taking action. In the eyes of God and law. *Who does the hard jobs? Not he who can…*

Barrett reached for the door handle and stepped out.

…but he who has nothing left to lose.

At least he had that going for him.

He was approaching the Air Stream, arranging words in his mind when the air behind him filled with the thunder of approaching Harleys.

Parley

MICK RODE in at the head of a half-dozen Paladins and braked to a stop directly in front of Barrett.

"Boo!" said Mick. But his expression was serious. "Guess I owe you an apology, father. I had you tailed."

Barrett glanced at the Air Stream. And immediately regretted it.

"That where they are?" Mick aimed the wheel of his hog in that direction.

"Wait." Barrett grabbed the handlebars of Mick's Harley. "Mick, please…"

Mick's eyes narrowed on Barrett's hand. He waited until the priest withdrew it to speak.

"Father…" Big Mick smirked, glanced at Pappy whose bike was immediately behind and to the right of his. "Listen, maybe you don't understand. You've never had kids. But where your blood is involved, when it's your kids? That's sacred. That's primal, man. It's also about pride. If Jackie's in there with Huns against her will, they've all got to die. It's that fucking simple. Now get the *fuck*"—he gunned the bike—"out of our way."

"Mick, Mick…hey. Listen."

"No! I'm done fucking listening to some priest. Anyway, this isn't any of your business. Don't think I won't fucking smoke you right here!" Mick flicked back his vest to reveal the grip of the pistol jammed in his belt. "God help me, I will. Now *move*."

"I will not."

Barrett's voice, emanating from deep in the black tunnel where the words were not truly his own, surprised even him.

Mick's hand went to his gun.

Barrett crossed himself. "Into thy hands, O Lord," he whispered.

He was ready. Here and now, he was ready to go in the service of a greater good.

Mick drew his gun partway out of his waistband and hesitated, doubt flickering across his bearded face. In an instant, Pappy had pulled up beside him, a hunting knife already partway from its sheath, murder in his eyes. "I'll take him, Mick…"

"No." Mick's eyed narrowed. "Father, I can't fucking believe you. You're a drunk and a loser, but you got balls of steel standing against ten mounted Paladins without even a fucking slingshot. Exactly what the fuck is it you're proposing here?"

"Fifteen minutes. Give me fifteen minutes in there, that's all. If I'm not out by then, come in, guns blazing. I don't care. But give me fifteen minutes to try and end this peacefully. In Christ's name."

Jesus, did I just say that?

Mick and Pappy sat motionless. Then…

"He's got a point, Mick." Pappy sheathed his knife slowly. "If nothing else, he might be able to pull Jackie out of the way before shit starts."

Barrett glared at Mick, daring him to disagree.

"Fifteen minutes." Mick's jaw firmed. "You got fifteen. Go."

Barrett turned and crossed the gravel to the Air Stream quickly. Reaching the door, he raised an arm and knocked. A woman in a housecoat with a scarf tied over her hair answered, opening just a crack and peering around the edge.

"I'm here to see Jackie."

"Oh?" Barrett's words obviously came as a surprise to her. "Who shall—"

"I'm Father Barrett from the parish of St. Michael's and St. Joan's. Jackie's father is a friend. She knows me."

The woman stared at Barrett slack-jawed for a time before turning and speaking to someone inside. Then she pulled the door wide and stepped away. As Barrett entered, he noted the sawed-off shotgun she held snout-down against her thigh. The door opened onto a small kitchen. At the table sat the Gigolo in a housecoat, engrossed in his cell-phone. A silver automatic lay beside the coffee cup and ash tray before him.

"They're in the living room." The man didn't look up or even acknowledge Barrett. The priest followed the woman with the housecoat and shotgun down the short companionway to the small common room of the trailer.

Deke sat on the couch. Despite doing his best to project an image of calm with his beer bottle and crossed legs, Barrett could tell he had heard the Harley thunder and was shaken. Same with the other three Huns in the room with him. And there was Jackie. Thigh-boots. Black leather miniskirt. Midriff tee and leather jacket, red hair freshly-styled retro punk. She sat with her legs crossed and an angry frown on her face, a cigarette smouldering between the first two fingers of her right hand as her left clenched and unclenched into a fist in her lap.

"Hello, Jackie."

"Father." Her tone was clipped, angry. "Here you are, huh? Just couldn't keep your nose out of it. Had to get involved. Do you feel better now? Now that you've caused all this trouble?"

"What trouble have I caused?"

She sniggered. "There's a dozen Harleys outside with Paladins on them. They wouldn't be here if you hadn't led them."

"And none of us would be here if we understood what was going on." Barrett moved in closer. All the seats were taken, so he crouched to look her in the eye. "Jackie, your father loves you and he's worried."

"*He's* worried?" She shook her head. "Jesus, that's rich. You hear that, babe?" She turned to Deke. "Mick's worried."

"Took him long enough," grumbled the blond biker.

"Mick's a monster, father." Jackie ground out her cigarette and lit a fresh one. "You have any idea what it's like growing up as the daughter of the Paladins' president? The people who don't worship you hate you. Even inside the club. And the moment you're old enough to fuck, suddenly you're the target of every wife and girlfriend figuring you're aiming to take their old man. I couldn't ever get away from it."

"Except when you went to the old Anglican cemetery." Barrett smiled softly. "To be with your friends. In high-school."

"What?" Her voice softened in wonder. "How did you know…"

"Scooter told me. Did you know the sexton at our church used to be your high-school janitor? He knew you, Jackie. Said you were a good kid. He was worried when you went missing. The whole town was."

She said nothing.

"RCMP were looking for you. Sergeant Lewis asked for my help. And that's why I'm here." Barrett pointed to Deke. "You're done being your daddy's little girl, is that it? You want to grow up and move on. Be your own person and be with the man you love."

Eyes averted, she nodded, slowly. It took Barrett a moment to notice the slow, thick tears sliding down her cheeks in absolute silence. When he spoke again, it was softly.

"So…what's this all about, Jackie? What the hell's been going on?"

Jackie drew shuddery breaths, like the sound a shovel makes digging up fresh earth from the forest floor. Still staring at the floor, she reached out and grasped Deke's hand. When she spoke, her voice was a dry husk.

"That Monday night. In the bar. That night you beat up Randy. That's when it started."

"Go on."

"I asked Randy to meet me there for a drink after work. I'd spent the weekend with Deke here and made a decision. It was time for Randy and me to end." She smirked. "That was the argument we were having at the Junction the night he hit me. The night you stepped in and Sergeant Gavin tazed you."

Deke and the other Huns elbowed one another and snickered.

Barrett flashed them the evil eye before muttering frostily, "Yes, I recall."

"I told Randy I'd found somebody else. I knew it was over between us. I wanted to tell him some place in public so I'd be safe because he wouldn't get violent, but he did. And then the Paladins got him…"

"And they killed him."

Jackie nodded. "That night. Grabbed him out of a car in a grocery store parking lot, dragged him into some field and shot him. Then they brought his body to our house. I didn't know whether to shit or go blind. And that's where I saw you again. Christ, padre. I can't believe you agreed to preside over his burial in the forest."

"You father gave me five thousand dollars. Plus I'm fairly sure he would have killed me if I refused."

Jackie's answering laugh was an ugly one. "Well so much for Christian fortitude."

"I can't be any good to the people here if I'm dead."

"You're not doing them much good alive."

"Touché." Barrett shrugged. "I'm trying to change that. That's why I'm here."

One of the Huns stood. He was a thin, mean-looking guy with a handlebar moustache. As Barrett watched, he pulled an Uzi out from under his chair.

"We'll go out there and we'll just end this now," said Handlebar Moustache. "It's what Hunter sent us to do in the first place. Now's our chance."

Jackie spun to him. "And *kill* my father?"

"I won't allow it."

All eyes turned to Barrett. And he was furious.

"Absolutely no goddam way I'm going to let you walk out of here and fire off a submachine-gun in a trailer park full of people. Your walking out that door is a guarantee a gunfight will happen, and these trailer walls are thin. A lot of people will die. No. You're not going."

Handlebar Moustache turned the Uzi on Barrett.

"Go ahead," Barrett snarled from the depths of the black

tunnel. "Seriously. I fucking dare you. Blow away a man of God in front of a room full of witnesses. The Catholic Church will hunt you down. And the arm of the Church is long. Though you run to the ends of the earth, they will find you. And they will bring the wrath of God down upon you because killing me is mortal sin, an offense against the Throne of Peter. And the hounds of the Inquisition, once loosed, cannot be called back. They will bring ruin down upon you and your entire family. Think about it."

Handlebar Moustache replied: "I'm giving you 'til five, father, to step aside. One."

"No."

"*Two.*"

Barrett stood his ground.

"Three!" The man snapped the safety off his machine-pistol. "Four!"

Jackie stood and moved to a point between Barrett and Handlebar Moustache. "Put the gun away, Tommy," she said tiredly.

"Move, Jackie."

"I said put it down. Do it."

Barrett heard some of Big Mick's steel in his daughter's voice and heaved a sigh of relief when the man called Tommy lowered the Uzi.

Jackie turned to Barrett. "I'll go out and talk to him." She shook her head. "Least I can do."

"You're a brave girl." Barrett was deeply impressed. "I'll go with you."

"I'd appreciate it." She flashed an annoyed look at Tommy. "Anything to avoid a showdown, a gunfight. You're right."

Together, they dismounted the Air Stream and began crossing the parking lot toward Mick.

"It was you, wasn't it?" Barrett asked. "You were the one who moved Randy's body. The Huns helped you."

"Deke and our friend Sam, the guy who owns the trailer. They helped me dig him up and get him to the funeral home, yeah. You told the Mounties?"

"Sure." Barrett sighed. "But the way I figure it, Randy was grabbed from his car by drug dealers who mistook him from someone else. That's what I'll tell Lewis I found out. Divert suspicion from your dad and your new friends in there." Barrett nodded back at the trailer. "One way or the other we'll get them—and you —out of town safely. I'll help Mick deal with it."

"Oh? That a service you offer? Besides drinking and fucking up in general?"

"An additional service rendered at no extra charge." Barrett crossed himself as they approached Mick and he began arranging words in his mind.

Dolan

SLOWLY, painfully Barrett trudged along the main drag, a box of wine dangling from his left arm, the receipt still wound into the cardboard aperture of the handle. He was dog-tired right down to his bones and wanted nothing more than return to his unit in the Fulton Arms Motor Hotel, turn out the lights, draw a bath, strip and sit in warm water up to his chin in the dark, listening through the half-open door to the television in the other room. It was, he decided, the celibate man's modest equivalent to a hero's welcome in a lady's arms but he felt he deserved it all the same.

But it would have to wait for now. Because Barrett had an important duty to discharge—one he had to deal with immediately.

He turned down the street which led to the parish house. Junk clogged the edge of the driveway and, Barrett could see, filled it right up to the open garage door where Father Dolan stood before his squadron of boats on boat trailers. Chests of drawers and full moving boxes had spilled out of the house onto the lawn. By all indications, Barrett's replacement was in obsessive hoarder heaven.

Barrett hoped Dolan had enjoyed his stay.

"Father Barrett." Dolan's tone was whispery, his manner distracted as he polished a chrome fixture on the rear of one boat. "Such a pleasant surprise to see you. I daresay, things have been going *very* well for us here at the church in your absence. So *much* to tell you. The parishioners have been very welcoming."

"Glad to see you, are they?" Barrett sighed and dug in a pocket for cigarettes. "You were happy to get back, I take it."

"Thanks be to God." Dolan crossed himself.

"You came back on…?"

"Friday. Morning."

"I see." Barrett smirked. "And you came right here?"

"Indeed, I did."

"Didn't you stop and get groceries?"

"That was later. Actually, a parishioner did it for me. I never left the house. As you can see, I have a great many personal possessions—"

"You've, ah, really settled in here, haven't you? Made yourself at home. Looks like you're planning to stay for a while."

At this, Father Dolan paused, and Barrett could sense the hesitation hovering in the air. And then Dolan was smiling and breaking that tension by straightening and setting aside his can of polish.

"Father Barrett, look." He smiled winsomely. "I understand it's a humiliation for a man of your, ah, *prior* stature to find himself forced into retiring from a post of prominence. I understand the feelings of self-doubt and diminishment you must be experiencing. I'm sure you saw this parish as your natural right, by virtue of your status as a high flier. But I think it's time you just faced it. You have been beaten. The better man has come along and replaced you. I'm sorry but there it is."

"In the morning, I'm phoning RCMP and telling them you were the one who broke Scooter's arm and spray-painted the church."

Dolan, eyes wide with shock, literally had to reach out and grasp something to remain upright. Barrett's words were a shock, alright.

"Yeah, I bet the locals are glad to see you. But not as glad as you were to see them that Thursday you rolled into town and started asking around about me. Found out all sorts of things, didn't you? Somehow you learned I was having trouble with the local native kids. So you took a trip down to McLellan's."

"What day was this?" Barrett could see Dolan figuring, counting backwards in his head.

"Last Thursday. The day before the Huns rolled into town. Morning of. You were in McLellan's."

"No, I wasn't…"

"Yes, you were. I saw you on CCTV. Bought yourself a coupla cans of spray paint and a black hoodie."

"I didn't arrive in town until—"

"Conserve your energy. You're going to need it moving out."

"Moving *out?*"

"Yep."

"Now, why would I do that?"

"Because if you don't, I'm going to tell Archbishop Crowe what I know. I am prepared to provide him with videotape, a statement, and an evidence package containing both cans of spray paint. They're a match to the paint used in the graffiti bombing and your prints are on them."

The last bit was a lie but Barrett could see Dolan had bought it hook, line, and sinker.

"What do you want?" Dolan whispered.

"You. Out. By sundown tomorrow. And all my stuff put back where it belongs. No excuses. Or it'll be Defrocking Drama at Archdiocese headquarters. Remember, I used to work for the Inquisition. Don't fuck with me, Dolan, or you'll burn at the stake."

With that, he turned on his heel and headed back to the motel.

Tally

"Yep."

It was quiet in the Junction. Barrett and Lewis held up the bar by themselves. An elderly couple munched hamburgers and fries out of plastic baskets and sipped dollar beer. The local seniors home would be in later. It was karaoke night. The karaoke lady was setting up her equipment at the DJ station.

"So…why did Father Dolan resign from his post again?"

"Dunno." Barrett shrugged innocently. "His e-mail mentioned personal health issues and requested a leave of absence. Archbishop Crowe's e-mail to me arrived ten minutes later. Guess I'm back in business as your local Catholic priest."

"Which reminds me." Lewis fished in a pocket and produced a cashier's check, which he pushed across the bar to Barrett. "For services rendered. You did an outstanding job. I'll definitely hire you again. Was going to add *'if you're still around'* but it looks like you will be."

"That I am!" Barrett slipped the check into his pocket and toasted Lewis. Along with the money he'd managed to save during his leave and the Paladins' five grand, Barrett figured he had enough to buy himself a treat.

Maybe I'll go on a cruise, he thought.

The karaoke lady had finished setting up. She switched on her microphone, tapped it and said, "Good evening." A moment later, rolling piano chords were gushing through the speakers and the lady was singing about a small-town girl, living in her lonely world. Lewis shook his head.

"So this is the kind of song the old folks karaoke to?"

Barrett shrugged. "We're getting old."

The door opened and Walton appeared with Ann Fletcher, Esquire in tow. They waved and wandered over, joining Barrett and Lewis at the bar.

"How'd the big case go?" Lewis gestured for the barman to set them up with a round on his tab.

"Good." Ann Fletcher, Esquire, yanked off her glasses, threw them down, and rubbed her eyes. "It was a tough case. Poaching cases usually are, but we won it. A great deal of credit goes to your Mr. Walton. He was our all-star witness, laying it on with that old school Ontario charm."

"Relic's been put away." Walton toasted Lewis with his beer when it came. "Bastard's finally going down. Five years. How did your big case end up?"

Lewis nudged Barrett. "I'll let my star investigator tell you."

Everyone turned to Barrett. He took a moment to compose himself and light a cigarette.

"Randy fell afoul of some dealers," he began. "Apparently they'd been scouting the area, recruiting customers in a bid to grab a piece of the action here. For whatever reason—perhaps he'd witnessed a deal or it was a case of mistaken identity or something—they pulled Randy from his car and, as near as I can tell, shot him and buried him in the woods." He glanced at Lewis. "This is where things get interesting.

"One of the dealers who participated in the hit is friends with Deke, who is dating Jackie on the sly. Now Randy and Jackie used to be a couple, so she still has fond feelings for him. Despite the fact that he used to drink too much and smack her around. Women are funny like that. No offense there, counsellor…"

"None taken." Ann Fletcher, Esquire, smirked and sipped her martini.

"Deke knew where the body was buried. Literally. So she and some friends rolled out there, dug him up and dumped him at the funeral home. Then she took off with Deke. And things escalated from there. And now here we are."

"The moral of the story being?" Lewis raised his eyebrows.

Barrett considered the karaoke lady for a long minute.

"Don't stop believing," he said at last.

Lewis groaned. Ann Fletcher, Esquire, snickered.

The door opened and an older man in a green ball-cap shuffled in. Barrett recognized the Chief. Seeing everyone at the bar, he wandered over.

"Hello," he said, pulling up a stool. He waved at the bartender, who immediately bent and opened a storage cupboard below the bottle display on the back wall. He drew out a stainless-steel mixer and cup attachment which he set up and tested. Barrett recognized it as one of those classic milkshake mixers. And, sure enough, the barkeep reached into the fridge to produce a carton of ice cream and a litre of whole milk. These he mixed together expertly, then spun in the mixer. He poured the result into a sundae glass and deposited it in front of the Chief.

"I'm diabetic," the Chief confessed, unwrapping a straw. "I can only do this every now and then. But today seemed a good day. My blood sugar is doing okay."

"Is that a milkshake?" Ann Fletcher, Esquire, squinted at the machine. "Can I have one?"

"Nope." The Chief smiled. "That's my private stash."

Barrett toasted him. "Cheers."

"Cheers, father."

"So. What are your plans for tonight?" Lewis directed this at Walton. But Fletcher answered.

"I lost a bet and have to buy nature boy here dinner." She slapped Walton's shoulder. "He wants surf and turf. Your CO is no cheap date, Lewis."

"How about yourself, Gavin?" asked Walton.

"Oh, a bit of paperwork. Then I'm going to go online and buy us a new hunting tent. Got some cash in…"

Behind his milkshake, the Chief chuckled to himself but said nothing.

"I'll be planning our next hunting trip. I'm thinking we should try for an elk."

"Ooh, hunting. Can I come?" asked Ann Fletcher, Esquire.

"Shit, no," replied Lewis. "Hunting's a man thing."

Walton laughed.

"What about you, father?" Ann Fletcher swirled her martini. "What are your plans?"

Barrett carefully considered everything he'd been through these past ten days or so. He weighed his resolve to become a better priest and community member against his own personal obstacles to faith. He wondered at the town of which he was now a part. And he realized he had no plan to face this complex future or to even answer the question.

"My plan for now," he said at last, "is to have another drink."

A Look at Book Two:
SINS OF THE FATHER

FATHER BARRETT IS BACK FOR BOOK TWO IN THIS SINISTER MYSTERY SERIES.

Ex-Vatican investigator Father Michael Barrett is still adjusting to life as parish priest in the backwater town of Fulton, British Columbia when he is called to the deathbed of Arnold McLellan—Fulton's wealthiest man.

Death is complicated at the best of times. But McLellan's heirs are at odds, and his main asset, the Spirit Ranch Estates development, is tied up in litigation with the local tribe. As a mysterious break-in at Barrett's parsonage coincides with the unexplained disappearance of First Nations youths, a series of clues tie the missing kids to the disputed estates. Too soon, Barrett finds himself torn between the roles of investigator and mediator in a brewing conflict between the tribe and the local townspeople.

Can Barrett race against the clock to find the missing kids while working to prevent the town from descending into total war?

AVAILABLE SEPTEMBER 2022

About the Author

Jamie Mason is the author of several science fiction novels and thrillers. Born in Montreal, he attended the University of Arizona and Chapman University. After a decade spent teaching in the southwest, he returned to Canada in 2005. He has worked variously as a think-tank analyst, a business manager, a professional musician and a private investigator. Now semi-retired and living in the woods of Vancouver Island, he devotes his time to writing and savoring the vanishing Canadian wilderness.